BOUND

Tribute Brides of the Drexian Warriors #6

TANA STONE

Broadmoor Books

Chapter One

S hreya came to slowly, straightening her neck and wincing at the ache.

Bloody hell. That's what she got for sleeping upright in a chair, she thought. As if she'd had much choice. She tugged at her wrists, not needing to look down to know they were bound to the armrests. Wiggling her fingers, she moved blood back into her hands after being immobile for who knew how long.

Blinking a few times, she focused on the dimly lit cockpit. Gray tiles that looked like scales covered the interior, and only a narrow slat of glass stretched in front of her—a reminder that she was in a vessel that was hurtling through space and away from the only home she knew and the only people she considered friends.

She swiveled her head, gradually looking over at the alien sitting in the pilot's seat. Big and muscular, with bronze skin, he was *not* a friend. He'd proven that when he'd abducted her from the Drexian ship she was on during a rescue attempt, and had cemented her opinion of him when he'd informed her that she had two choices: mate with him or die.

Shreya barely contained her derisive laugh. This guy was in for a surprise if they thought those were her only two options. She'd survived a tsunami on Earth, which had claimed the rest of her family and had been kidnapped by aliens once before. She'd persevered through both and come out stronger. She'd even managed to carve out a life for herself on the space station the Drexians had brought her to, living with the other human women who'd declined to be mated to one of the hunky Drexian alien warriors. She was considered an "independent," which suited her just fine. This, she thought, as she shifted in the firm chair, was merely a setback.

Her mind flashed to her friend, Ella, another independent who'd been on the rescue mission with her. She hoped the woman was safe, and the Drexians—who'd gone into the Kronock research facility looking for the hybrid cyborg she was now with—had gotten out unscathed. And, maybe more importantly, she really hoped they were coming after her.

Watching his fingers move across the console, Shreya noticed his one red, cybernetic eye blinking. If she didn't want to kick him in the balls so badly, she would have loved to be able to study the metal implant that curved around his temple and eye socket. Her field of study was microbiology—at least it had been before she'd been abducted from her university in the UK—but the scientist in her couldn't help but be curious about the advanced machinery in his head, and how it worked with his biology.

The irony was, she'd been on the Drexian rescue ship to rescue *him*. He'd been captured by the Kronock and infused with their DNA to make him into a hybrid of the two species. So not only was he given a cybernetic eye like some of the Kronock warriors had, his skin had grown gray scales in uneven patches. She'd studied what they'd done to him from records one of the Drexian warriors had taken from the Kronock and determined that the DNA splicing wasn't stable. As a matter of fact, she'd been prepping to restore his original DNA when he'd boarded the ship and knocked her out. If the rescue mission had succeeded, he would have been the one tied up, and she would have been helping him regain his Drexian DNA and life.

Unfortunately, the plan had gone sideways. Her friend, Ella, had left the ship to warn the Drexian team about a possible ambush, and somehow the hybrid had eluded them and snuck onto the ship. Now, they were on an enemy ship flying somewhere, and she suspected it was far away from her friends and the Drexian space station.

He swung his head toward her. "You're awake."

Shreya shrank back, startled by his sudden movement. Although he sounded mostly Drexian—his deep voice only slightly halting—the pulsing red of his eye reminded her instantly he was not. Not anymore.

"That's good." He looked forward again.

She cleared her throat. "Where are you taking me?"

After a moment's pause, he tapped a star chart on the computer console. "Lymora III."

"That means nothing to me. In case you haven't noticed, I'm human. We don't travel to different planets like you guys do."

He tilted his head at her. "And how do we do?"

"Like you're driving around the block," she said. "I've heard other Drexians talk about visiting planets like we visit the market."

"I am not Drexian."

She didn't answer. He may have been programmed by the Kronock to think he wasn't Drexian, but nearly every bit of him —from his chocolate-brown hair to his one sea-green eye, to the raised nodes running down his spine—looked Drexian. It didn't help his argument that he was shirtless, except for open-sided armor slung over his shoulders, and she could see that his sculpted chest muscles and chiseled abs were covered in skin, not scales.

"So what's Lymora III?" she asked, deciding to leave the Drexian identity crisis for another time. "A Kronock-occupied planet?"

His fingers hesitated as they hovered over the star chart. "No. I've decided not to take you to a Kronock facility."

She remained quiet, hoping he would want to fill the silence. Nothing. Whether he was Drexian or Kronock, he was clearly the strong, but silent, type.

"Why not?" she finally asked.

He shifted in his chair without looking over. "I do not prefer the lab. It is cold and too bright. Some things should not be done there."

"Like?"

"I have been tasked with finishing General Krav's plan." His voice took on a strange tone, as if he was reading from a script. "I will fulfill my duty, but I will do it my own way."

"So you're a rebel," she said under her breath. "I'll bet there aren't many of those among the Kronock."

He darted a glance at her. "You are not what I expected."

"No? Am I the first human you've ever met?"

"Yes, although I have heard much about your species." His gaze dropped to her chest for a moment. "You are smaller than I expected."

"I'm considered petite." She felt a need to defend herself. "But all humans are smaller than Drexians. Or Kronock."

"And your skin is a similar shade to mine," he continued. "I'd heard some Earthlings were so light they looked like the underbelly of a Carthian slug."

That didn't sound like a good thing. It hadn't always been an advantage, but at the moment, Shreya felt grateful for the warm brown of her skin. Since she'd met aliens with blue, purple, and green skin, the variations in human skin color seemed less significant.

"So you've heard all about humans, but have never met one before me?" She remembered hearing something once about the importance of humanizing yourself to a kidnapper. "My name is Shreya."

There was a long pause before he answered. "I am Vox."

She didn't ask if that was his Drexian name, or a new Kronock name he'd been given. "So, you've never been to the space station for tribute brides? You've never seen the Boat?"

A brusque shake of his head. "Never, but I know that human females are very important to the Drexians."

"Tell me about it." Shreya let out a breath. "I heard the whole spiel when I was kidnapped from Earth and brought up to the Boat. Your species stopped producing females, so you were searching for compatible mates and you happened upon Earth. The Kronock were about to invade, but the Drexians made a deal to provide protection in exchange for a small number of women each year. Yadda yadda yadda." She made a circling gesture with one restrained hand. "That's how I ended up being taken. Apparently, I'm part of the fifty percent of females who're compatible. Unfortunately, I had no desire to marry a total stranger, so I declined the offer of becoming a tribute bride."

His head snapped up. "You are not a tribute bride?"

"Nope. I'm what the others on the station call 'rejects' but we call ourselves 'independents'."

"I was supposed to capture a tribute bride."

"Then you might as well let me go," Shreya said. "I promise you, I'm not one of them."

He narrowed his one eye at her. "But you are human, and you just told me you are compatible with Drexians, which means you are compatible with me. That is what is most important."

So much for that.

"You know they're going to find you," she said, trying a different tack. "The Drexians won't let you get away with taking a human, even if I'm not a tribute bride. And my friend, Ella, definitely won't let it go. They'll be coming after us."

"They won't find you." He didn't look over. "I removed your tracker when I knocked you out, so they won't be able to use that. This is a Kronock ship, not easily traced by Drexians. Plus, I'm taking you somewhere they would never expect to find you."

Shreya's stomach tightened. "Is Lymora III some sort of waste-land, where we'll have to wear gas masks to survive?"

"No." He flicked his fingers across the console, and the ship begin to decelerate. "It is a pleasure planet on the far outskirts."

"A pleasure planet?" Her mouth gaped open. "Are you taking me to an alien version of a bordello?"

"I do not know this 'bordello', but if it is a place where you can indulge in pleasures of the flesh and engage in any act you can imagine without judgment, then, yes. I am taking to the roughest and most notorious bordello in the galaxy." His red eye flickered as he looked at her. "A place the Drexians would never expect."

Shreya swallowed hard.

Chapter Two

Vox set the ship down carefully, watching the dust kick up around them. His ship was only one of many docking near the capitol city; the planet was as busy as usual. In the distance and through the haze, he saw the outlines of buildings with squared-off roofs, and the occasional mushroom dome. A small, red sun glowed in the sky, its distant rays doing little to cut through the thick atmosphere.

Aliens with cloth wrapped over their faces scurried around on the ground, recording data about his ship in their computerized arm bands, and he recognized them as the native Lymorans. Short, squat creatures with nearly translucent skin and no body hair, they were rarely seen uncovered.

Lymora III didn't have much to offer as a planet aside from its lack of rules and abundance of pleasure houses—for both males and females. After severe overpopulation centuries ago that depleted its natural resources and sent the plant into climate crisis, the planet had suffered from almost total species collapse. The Lymorans who had survived had learned to live on a planet with an arid climate and virtually no arable land. They'd taken the palaces of the former oligarchs and turned them into pleasure houses, creating a destination with no extradition laws, and no rules against prostitution, gambling, or smuggling.

The corner of Vox's lip curled up. The Drexian buried deep within him was repulsed by the lawlessness of the place, but he also knew that no one would blink twice at a bound female. Her screams would be ignored, or mistaken for part of a sex game. No one would send word to the Drexians because no one who frequented Lymora III wanted the honorable warrior race descending on the planet.

He rotated his chair to face her. "You may scream when we disembark, but I would prefer you do not. There is no point." She raised an eyebrow, and he continued. "Lymora III welcomes human trafficking and slave labor, so your cries for help will be ignored, or laughed at. I suggest you do not waste your breath."

The female glanced out the front of the ship. "Charming."

"Also, there is no guarantee that your cries wouldn't awaken the blood lust of a visiting Xakden, and you do not want one of them after you." He didn't want to fight off a Xakden in heat, either, although their outrageously engorged phalluses usually slowed them down enough to make it a fair fight. If there were only one of them.

Her golden-brown skin paled. "Blood lust?"

"Do not worry. It is only activated by the sounds of screaming, which is why I suggest you do not do it."

"Let me get this straight? If I scream I might cause some scary alien to come after me?" She narrowed her eyes at him. "That's a pretty convenient story for you."

He shrugged, pulling a pair of blades off the wall behind her and attaching them to his belt. "I am only telling you the truth." He leaned down so that their faces were only inches apart. "I promise you, human, you are much better off mating with me, than being fucked by a Xakden. With me, you will not be ripped in two."

She inhaled sharply and her pupils widened. "You don't scare me."

He leaned back, studying the tears that filled her eyes. "I think I do, but I am not who you need to be afraid of."

"Really?" Her voice quavered, but had an edge to it. "So I'm not supposed to be afraid of the guy who knocked me out, kidnapped me, tied me up, and now plans to force himself on me?"

Vox flinched at her words. He would never do those things. No honorable Drex—. He shook his head, the General's echoing voice in his mind as he recalled the jolts of electricity that made his body convulse until he'd lost consciousness. No. He was no longer a Drexian. He was Kronock, and he had a mission to complete.

He fisted his hands. "You do not understand."

"I could never understand you." She met his gaze, her eyes blazing. "Not what you've become. You're a monster."

Somewhere in the deep recesses of his mind, he felt an urge to defend himself, to prove he wasn't a monster. Irrelevant, he thought, Krav's voice becoming his own. It doesn't matter what she thinks of you. There is only the mission.

He reached down and untied her hands, pulling her to standing and spinning her around without releasing her arms. Binding her hands together again behind her, Vox turned her back around and steered her forward by the elbow. "This monster did not take you to a lab, where they would have strapped you to a table and impregnated you with the hybrid they need. So, perhaps, there are worse monsters out there?"

"You want me to thank you for that?" Her laugh was hard and mirthless. "You're still going to force yourself on me, right? I mean, that's the whole point. Now you're just going to do it in an alien whorehouse. I don't think that makes you some kind of hero."

Again, her words stung, and he tried to ignore the impulses they stirred up. He had no idea a human female would be so difficult. He'd imagined that the small, fragile creature would be compliant and willing once she understood the situation, but this one was not. Vox sighed as they reached the center of the ship. "Do you always argue this much?"

She laughed again, this time louder. "When I'm being kidnapped? Always."

He shook his head as he pulled a pair of heavy, brown cloaks out of a cabinet, throwing one over his shoulders and then draping one over hers. He flipped up both hoods and started to pull the fabric veil across her face.

She jerked away. "What are you doing?"

He frowned, closing in on her as she backed up until she was flush against the wall, his own, much larger, body nearly touching her. Vox suddenly realized how pretty she was when she was angry. His bionic eye quickly computed her biological reactions, projecting a read-out into his brain. Her body temperature was elevated, her breathing was ragged, and her pupils were so wide that her warm brown eyes looked nearly black—the same physical reactions most females had when they were aroused. She tipped her head back to meet his eyes, and her tongue licked her lower lip.

His cock twitched. Was it possible she was also aroused? He traced a finger down her cheek as he retrieved the corner of the veil. "This will keep the dust out of your mouth."

"Oh," she whispered, trembling as he touched her.

He dragged his thumb over her bottom lip, the blood pounding in his ears and reminding him that only a very small part of him was cybernetic. A much bigger part was one hundred percent organic.

"I was on the list for a tribute bride," he said, his eyes riveted to hers. "Before."

She swallowed, but didn't respond, her own breath rapid.

"I'd never seen a human female, though. Not in person. Only images, and they don't do justice to how small and soft you are." He cupped her chin in his palm. "You feel so good. I wonder how you taste?"

As he lowered his mouth to hers, he was vaguely aware of her leg quickly moving up. Before he could react, a blinding flash of pain knocked him to the ground, and he clutched his groin. She'd managed to knee him in the balls. Vox would have been impressed if he weren't in so much pain.

He could hear her running past him, and he threw out an arm, catching her by the ankle and bringing her down hard.

"Bloody bastard," she cried as she awkwardly hit the steel floor, her hands still tied behind her back. She attempted to scoot away from him.

Crawling to all fours, his balls still aching, Vox reached her and rolled her over so she was facing up. "You attacked me."

Even though tears streaked her cheeks, her eyes still flashed defiantly. "You attacked me first."

"So you were getting even with me?"

"We aren't even close to even," she said. "But consider that a thank you for knocking me out before."

"I can see you're not going to make this easy," he muttered to himself.

"You're two for two, asshat."

Asshat? Even though he had a universal translator implant, that word did not make any sense to him. He didn't know what it meant, although he suspected it was not flattering—but he did not have time for more talking. The Lymorans who collected the entry tax would be waiting for him, as would the suite he'd reserved in the most private pleasure house.

Standing, he picked her up and tossed her over his shoulder, hooking an arm behind her knees and holding them firmly, so she could not kick him again. He ignored her yelps as he opened the ship's hatch, giving her ass a firm slap and covering his own head and face before descending down the ramp.

Even with the heavy fabric shielding his mouth, Vox could taste the acrid dust that hung in the air. He paused at the bottom of the ramp, handing the waiting Lymoran a pair of shiny Allurian gold pieces and watching the short alien rub them between his fat fingers.

"Always a pleasure to do business with the Kronock Empire," the Lymoran said in a gravelly voice that was surprisingly deep for one so small. He merely glanced at the figure wiggling on Vox's shoulder. "Enjoy your visit to Lymora III."

Vox nodded and strode off without making eye contact with the other arriving aliens, although he made note of them. No Drexians. Not that he expected to see any. They had no way to track him or her anymore, and no reason to think they were on a lawless pleasure planet on the outskirts of the galaxy.

No. The Drexians would fruitlessly search the many Kronock outposts and colonies, while he stayed hidden here with the human. Safe and secret while he completed his mission.

His bionic eye searched through the dusty air and located the mushroom dome of his destination, effortlessly calculating the distance and shortest route. His heart beat faster as he thought of the suite awaiting them, and felt the human moving restlessly. Vox slapped her ass once more, enjoying the way the soft flesh quivered beneath his hand, and quickened his pace.

Chapter Three

I t was pointless for her to try and memorize the path Vox was taking, especially from her upside down vantage point. Shreya lifted her head, trying to take in the brown, stone buildings as they moved down streets and through passageways, but the air was hazy and she suspected he was taking a roundabout route.

She concentrated on not sucking in too much of the dusty air, and trying to keep from bouncing against his wide back. It was humiliating to be carried upside down, not that any of the aliens on the planet could see her face through the thick cloak and the fabric draped across the lower part of her face. She'd given up squirming on his shoulder, since it really had no effect, but she wiggled her legs every so often to keep them from going numb. Usually the wiggling got her a sharp slap on the ass, so she didn't do it often.

From the sounds and smells, Lymora III appeared to be a bustling place—and a seedy one. Music drifted out from bars they passed— sometimes slow and sultry and sometimes fast and pulsating—as well as laughter and catcalls, and it wasn't difficult to imagine women dancing to the beat on stages and around poles. The stale scent of alcohol wafted up from the ground, and Shreya wondered how many drinks had been spilled on these streets. As Vox side-stepped a dark stain on the paving stones, she wondered what else had been spilled there, and her stomach tensed. Blood, perhaps?

As they wound down narrower passageways and tight alleys, the sounds faded and the smells subsided. No longer were they surrounded by the footfall of the crowd. It was almost eerily quiet, as Vox stopped and pounded on a door. Muffled bells chimed from inside, and Shreya heard the door groan as it was opened with great effort.

"I am expected," he said, as he walked inside and onto the tiled floor.

The door was closed again and a bolt thrown. Shreya shook her head, slightly dislodging the veil and head covering, and inhaled deeply, grateful that the air inside was clean, even if it did smell like being inside a sachet filled with cloves and cinnamon.

"You can put me down now," she said, swiveling her head around. "They locked the door."

Vox grunted and swung her down from his shoulder, setting her upright and appraising her with a cursory glance. He tugged her head coverings completely off. "It is pointless to attempt to escape from here."

Shreya looked back at the towering, arched door that looked like it was made from stone and had a wide metal bolt across it. A massive, furry alien with arms like tree trucks, hooves for feet, and a long tail stood next to it. She assumed it was this black-furred giant's job to drag the door opened and closed, and she swallowed hard when she noticed him breathing heavily from the recent exertion. Vox was right. No way was she getting the door open on her own.

She took in the rest of the circular foyer, with its gleaming, white-tiled floor, and delicate gilded tables arranged around the walls, topped with high, ornately carved mirrors. Doors were tucked between the tables, but there were no knobs.

"We are honored the Kronock would visit our house." A high, singsong voice came from above, and Shreya pivoted to watch the owner of the voice descend a sweeping staircase.

The stairs wound up several stories, and she had to tip her head back to see the pointed tip of the mushroom-shaped dome that topped the building. Light seemed to stream inside from the dome, illuminating the brightly painted interior, and highlighting the painted scenes of lush, naked women in various stages of embrace with a variety of aliens. She tried not to gasp audibly at the enormous equipment depicted on some of the aliens, and hoped the artist had been trying to flatter the clientele.

Shreya pulled her gaze from the murals to focus on the woman who seemed to float down toward her. She did a quick double-take when she realized the woman was indeed floating, because she had a small pair of wings fluttering behind her that kept her hovering about a foot off the ground. Her hair was a soft shade of lilac, and fell in waves around her shoulders, and her eyes were the exact same shade but turned up in an exotic slant with long lashes that she blinked languidly. She stared curiously at Shreya.

"Zylia," Vox said, nodding at the creature, as she hovered briefly in front of him.

Zylia left him and rotated around her. "She's lovely. What is she?"

"Human," Vox said. "From planet Earth."

"Fascinating." The woman leaned closer and fluttered her eyelashes. "I've never seen a Drexian mate before." She cut her eyes to Vox. "I will pay you handsomely for her."

Vox shook his head and shot his hand out to clasp Shreya's arm. "She's not for sale. She is the property of the Kronock. No one will touch her but me."

Shreya was about to protest that she was *not* the property of the Kronock, and he was going to touch her over her dead body, but she decided to remain silent. Being sold to a brothel just might be worse, if the murals overhead were any indication.

The winged alien shrugged. "As you wish. Of course, we would never want to anger the Kronock empire, but if you tire of her, I have many clients who would find a human exotic."

Shreya couldn't help the shudder that passed through her. She'd definitely been places where her brown skin and dark hair had been considered exotic, but this was a whole new level. As a creature without wings, fur, or scales, *she* was the one who was considered odd on this planet.

"Just our suite," Vox said. "The one I reserved."

"Yes, we made the special additions, as requested." Zylia smiled, her eyes sliding to Shreya again. "I am only sorry I will not get to watch."

Shreya took a small step closer to Vox. Despite Zylia's beauty, the winged creature made her nervous.

Zylia clapped her hands, and a tiny alien hurried into the foyer through one of the doors that seemed to swing open without her touching it. She barely reached Shreya's waist, and wore her pink hair swept up into a towering pile of curls that added at least another foot in height. Her skin was an iridescent blue that changed color in the light, and her face was garishly made up so that she looked almost like a china doll. Her dress belled out from her waist in a cascade of ruffles, reminding Shreya of a blue-skinned Little Bo Peep.

Zylia flicked her gaze over the small woman. "Show them to their special suite."

The small woman started up the staircase, waving them with her, as Zylia flew through one of the doors off the foyer.

Shreya cast a final glance at the door and the hulking guard before Vox tugged her by the arm, and they both fell in step behind the bobbing pink curls. When they reached the first landing, several heads popped out of the doors ringing the circular staircase.

"You brought us a new girl, handsome?" one of the women called out, holding her diaphanous robe closed with one webbed hand as she leaned out of a room.

"We don't need more competition, Cerise," another voice yelled at the tiny woman.

"She's not here to work," the small, pink-haired creature said, cutting them off with a snap of her fingers and without breaking her stride. "Least, not for coin."

Laughter and a few whoops followed them as they climbed another flight of curved stairs, and Shreya tried to ignore the burning of her cheeks. Vox didn't say a thing, but she felt him tense next to her, his fingers tightening slightly on her arm.

When they'd reached the top floor, Cerise led them to a gold door, pressing her hand against the surface. It beeped and swung open, and she stood aside, dropping her gaze as Vox entered and pulled Shreya behind him.

The suite was every bit as ornate as the rest of the building, with a high, inset ceiling, and gilded mirrors adorning the curved walls. A huge bed dominated the far side, with sheer, crimson fabric draped from its four gold posters, and fat, velvet pillows piled high along the back.

Shreya's mouth went dry when she spotted the straps attached the bedposts. She looked away, but her eyes landed on contraption hanging from the ceiling in one corner, that looked like it was a collection of straps and handles suspended from a heavy chain. She'd never seen one in person, but she felt pretty sure she was looking at an alien's version of a sex swing. Next to that was a giant

"X" mounted to the wall with straps at the top and bottom of each crossed beam. Again, not something she'd ever seen in person before, but she was pretty sure it was called a St. Andrew's cross. What kind of place was this?

Vox untied her, and she wrenching her arm away from him and backed away. Shreya looked desperately at the door, catching a sympathetic glance from Cerise as the creature stood in the hall and the door slid shut.

She balled her hands into tight fists and turned to face the hybrid cyborg. If he thought he was going to tie her up to some kinky piece of furniture, the guy had a serious fight on his hands.

Chapter Four

Vox studied her stance. Even though she was small and lithe, and no match for his bulk, he realized that she was preparing to fight him. She had spirit, he would give her that. Somewhere, in the depth of his brain, he registered that this was humorous. There was a time he would have thrown his head back and laughed.

Instead, he tilted his head at her. "You wish to engage me in battle, human?"

"I'm not going to let you tie me up or put me in that thing." She jerked her head toward the hanging contraption without breaking eye contact with him, then her gaze went to the enormous X. "Or on that."

His bionic eye automatically sized her up and registered her as no threat—small stature, slight muscle mass, no weapons. Not that he needed an implant to know that. If he wished to bind her to the bed or hang her from the ceiling, she would have no choice. He was significantly stronger and larger than her, and he was there to fulfill his mission. "Is that so?"

She nodded, and he saw that her shoulders were shaking.

As he thought about his mission, he heard General Krav's guttural voice in his head, repeating the words over and over in Kronock. *Capture an Earthling. Create a Kronock-human hybrid. Extract the hybrid DNA. Invade Earth. Infest the population with the hybrid DNA. Harvest the planet.*

He twitched, vaguely remembering a time when he fought against Kronock invasion. That was before he'd learned of the superiority of the Kronock empire. When he'd been a soft-hearted Drexian. Now he was a loyal Kronock soldier. A pain shot through his head, and he put a hand to his temple and cursed himself for his weak, Drexian body. The pains were increasing, but he could not let them alter his mission. He also did not feel up to a fight.

"I am not going to restrain you at this time."

Her arms dropped a bit. "Oh? Then what's with the sex dungeon stuff?"

He crossed to a table arranged with colorful glass bottles filled with equally colorful liquids, and pulled the stopper from a pink bottle shaped like an hourglass. Pouring several fingers worth of the Noovian whiskey into a short tumbler, he swirled the green drink in the glass before looking up.

"I hope it will be unnecessary." He flicked a glance to the swing and X-cross. "I was not specific in my requests. Zylia used her discretion."

Her eyes narrowed as she watched him, as if she was prey tracking her hunter. "Well, Zylia can sod off."

Vox grinned and tossed back the whiskey, comforted by the familiar burn that lessened the pain in his head. Memories of drinking with his former Drexian crewmates lurked hazily in his mind, as well as faint recollections of drinking with alien females before taking them to bed. He had never needed to force a female before and, despite his orders, he did not want to force this one.

He'd requested a suite with restraining devices—in case the human resisted—but had not known what Zylia would provide. Looking at the contraptions and imagining the small human strapped to them made his cock throb. He was glad he was facing away from her so she would not have additional reason to be scared.

He glanced back at her, her thick, black hair cascading over her shoulders, and her dark eyes large. He was no expert on Earth females, but he found this one to be very attractive. His eyes drifted lower to her body. Even though it was completely covered, it didn't take much imagination to see the curve of her breasts beneath her shirt. He knew humans had only two of them, and that they were known for being soft. His cock ached even more.

He did not want to force her to mate with him. His Drexian pride and honor may have been buried deep, but it could never be eradicated, even if he did not know why he felt the way he did. He wanted her to want him. He needed her to want it as much as he did, and he did not care if this delayed his mission. The Kronock did not need to know.

She cleared her throat, and his gaze snapped back to her face, lingering for a moment on her plump lips. Vox took a deep breath and willed his cock to relax. He poured another drink, this time an orange liquid from a tall cylinder, and walked it over to her. "Drink this."

She crossed her arms over her chest. "No thanks."

"You are not thirsty?"

"I'm not in the mood to be drugged."

His gaze flicked to the glass. "This is not drugged." He extended it again. "I promise."

"Then you drink it."

Vox sighed before taking a sip. He did not prefer the sweetness of the beverage, but he thought she would.

She eyed him as he swallowed and held the glass out to her, then finally took it, holding it but not drinking from it.

"I have no intention of drugging you or tying you up," he said. "I do not want to force you."

She gave a small snort of laughter. "Right. You kidnap me, tell me I have to mate with you, carry me here over your shoulder, bring me to a room decked out for bondage, and then say you aren't going to force me?"

Vox ran a hand over the scales on his arm, scratching at the place they met his flesh. "That is correct."

She took a tiny sip. "Forgive me if I'm not eager to believe you."

He turned and walked back to refill his glass. "I forgive you."

She laughed again. "Which part of you doesn't get sarcasm, the Drexian or the Kronock?"

Vox paused with his hand on the neck of the whiskey bottle, trying to separate the thoughts and voices battling in his head. It was hard to tell anymore what was Kronock and what was Drexian.

"Never mind," she said. "That was a hypothetical question."

He poured himself another drink, and saw that she had drunk half of hers. Downing his drink in a single, long gulp, he let the bitterness of the whiskey scorch his throat, and savored the warmth that filled his belly. His fingers buzzed and his shoulders relaxed, and he felt desire awaken in his core.

"I will make you a promise," he said, setting the glass down and walking toward her.

She blinked up at him. "Why should I believe any promise you make?"

"You do not have to believe me, but I will give you my word as a Dre—" he faltered, shaking his head and clearing his throat. "I give you my word."

She gazed up at him, glancing at his bionic eye and flinching slightly before focusing on his real one. "Okay."

As Vox stared down at the small creature—close enough for him to smell the sweet scent of her hair—need coursed through him. He could take her now. Pick her up and carry her to the bed and claim her. He wouldn't even need to restrain her with the straps, as her struggles would be easily overpowered by his considerable size and strength. The thought of burying his cock in her made him almost lightheaded with desire.

He knew what General Krav would have told him. Take her. Dominate her. Make her scream. Enjoy her fear. She is yours. That was the mission.

Vox shook his head to rid himself of the Kronock voice. No. He didn't want her that way. He knew what he had to do, but he would do it his way.

"I will not force you," he said, feeling her warm breath, quick and shallow. "I will only claim you when you ask me to."

Her eyebrows rose. "Then that's never going to happen."

Vox brushed a hair off her face, his fingertip grazing her cheek. "You will want me to take you."

"You're pretty cocky." Her pupils flared. "But, I'm never going to want that."

"We will see," he whispered.

"So you're not going to touch me until I tell you to?" she asked, her voice shaky.

He cupped her chin in his hand. "I did not say that." He rubbed his thumb across her jawbone. "I plan to run my hands and mouth over every bit of you. In time."

She gasped and jerked back. "No fucking way."

Vox shot a hand around her back to keep her from running, grasping a fistful of her shirt and pulling her flush to him. "We could always do it the other way. No one will interrupt us, no matter how much you scream."

Her breathing was ragged, and her gaze darted to the contraption in the corner. "So you're telling me it will only go as far as foreplay?"

"What is foreplay?"

Her cheeks reddened. "Kissing, touching, you know. All the stuff leading up to sex."

His heart hammered in his chest. "Until you tell me you want more. Then I will give you more."

She steadied her breath and met his eyes. "So you promise that unless I tell you to, you won't…?"

He hesitated for a moment, wondering if he should make such a promise. His entire mission depended on him impregnating her. Wanting her to be a willing partner was a luxury he knew he shouldn't allow. It was one General Krav would have scoffed at. Then again, Krav had never felt the rush of desire flaring in a female's eyes as he claimed her. Vox had, and knew there was nothing like it in the universe. The part of him that was not bionic needed her to want him as much as he wanted her.

He felt his resolve harden as he leaned close to her ear. "I promise I will not fuck you until you beg me, pretty human."

He heard her breath hitch in her chest, as he nipped her neck.

"Okay, then," she whispered. "It's a deal. But my name is Shreya. Not 'pretty human.'"

He repeated the name in his head, the sounds strange and soft to his tongue. "Fine, then, Shreya. You are probably eager to get out of those clothes."

"Not real—" she began.

"I arranged for something more fitting for you to wear." He crossed to a door set in one of the walls and slid it open, revealing a closet with garments hanging within. He pulled out a diaphanous, white dress knotted at the shoulders that draped in sheer layers.

When he turned around, holding it out, she was already shaking her head. "That's like a see-through toga."

He glanced at it as he walked toward her. "I do not know what a toga is, but this will look nice on you."

She folded her arms over her chest. "I'm fine in what I have on, thanks."

He frowned and cast a glance at the giant X. "I'm happy to tie you up and undress you."

Her eyes skittered to the straps on the crossed beams, and she snatched the dress out of his hands. "Fine."

She made a beeline for the open bathroom door, and he watched as she slammed it behind her. Vox did not mind a female with a little spirit. It would make it all the better when she finally submitted to him.

Chapter Five

Shreya leaned her back against the door of the bathroom once she'd closed it, cursing when she saw that the chamber had no windows. She shouldn't have expected any. Vox may have been part machine, but he wasn't stupid, and she doubted very much the alien fairy that ran the place was, either.

Grateful that she was alone and away from the imposing and watchful alien, she tossed the dress on the long vanity. She may have to wear it eventually, but she wasn't putting it on until the last possible moment. Being in the bathroom should buy her a few minutes, at least.

At least there was nothing creepy in here, she thought. No straps or harnesses. Just lots of cream-colored stone, and a few matching towels draped on hooks.

Her gaze went to the corner where what looked like a larger circular shower head extended down from the ceiling over a single drain in the floor. No shower doors, and only a few buttons on the wall she assumed were controls.

Shreya felt the day's grime on her, as she cast a nervous glance at the door. It didn't appear to lock, but he wouldn't interrupt her in here, would he?

"Screw it," she whispered to herself, pulling off her clothes and tossing them onto the counter next to the dress. She was dying for a shower.

Stepping under the shower head, she cautiously pressed one of the buttons. Nothing. Frowning, she tried another, and water began cascading from the ceiling. Freezing water. She danced away from the stream with a small yelp, darting her hand to the buttons again, jabbing anything in her attempt to warm it.

Momentarily, the water heated and the room began to smell like a bag of potpourri. She stepped back under the stream. Not only was the water gloriously hot, it was scented and slightly slick. She rubbed her arms and saw the water bead. Leave it to an alien brothel to add scented oil to the water.

Shreya let out a small moan of contentment as she let the water pour over her, leaning her head back and feeling it cascade down her face and hair. With her eyes closed, she could almost imagine she was back on the Boat in her own shower.

"Turn around."

His deep voice made her eyes fly open, and she flattened herself against the wall with a scream.

"What the hell are you doing in here?" she yelled. "Get out!"

"I'm watching you."

She swiped at her face in an attempt to get the oily water out of her eyes, but didn't turn to look at him. "You can't just walk in on me in the bathroom like a pervert. That wasn't part of the deal."

"Would you rather I touch you? I could assist in your cleaning."

She shook her head. "No. I don't need help. Can you please go?"

"I enjoy watching."

Now, she twisted her head to see him leaning against the counter, his long legs stretched out in front of him and crossed at the ankles. His arms were propping him up on the counter, and the huge bulge in his pants was unmistakable. "I'll bet you do."

"If you are done, I can assist you in dressing."

She pressed the wall buttons until the water flow stopped, and then crossed her arms over her breasts as she turned. "I can dress myself, thanks."

He pulled a towel from a nearby hook, and handed it to her as he stood.

Snatching it from his hand, she quickly wrapped it around her chest. She moved toward her discarded pants and shirt, but he blocked her, holding out the nearly sheer dress instead.

"I've worn hospital gowns with more coverage than that," she said, wrinkling her nose at the garment.

"Your other clothes are not practical," he said.

She pushed a dripping strand of hair off her forehead. "Pants and a button-down shirt aren't practical?"

"Not for my purposes."

She swallowed hard as he extended the dress to her. It didn't take a huge amount of intellect to understand his purposes.

Shreya hesitated, and he grabbed her wrist. "Fine. We will do it my way."

"Wait." She leaned back as he propelled her out of the bathroom and across the room toward the giant X. "I'll put it on."

He dragged her closer to the huge, flat beams with straps at the corners. "You had your chance, human."

Jerking against his large hands seemed to have no effect on the alien. He was too strong. Panic clawed at her throat when they reached the apparatus, and he strapped one of her wrists to the top.

"You don't need to do this," she said, straining against his grip as he tugged her other arm into place and fastened the restraint over it.

"That is where you are wrong," he said, his breathing heavy. "You must submit to me. That is the mission. Krav failed to keep the human female and bend her to his will, but I will not."

She wasn't sure exactly what he was talking about, but she had heard some whisperings on the Boat about one of the tribute brides being taken by the Kronock. Maybe that was the female this Krav had failed to keep.

The towel slipped from her body and dropped to the floor, leaving her exposed with her wrists bound to the top of the giant X. Oily water dripped down from her hair and mingled with the tears she felt squeezing out of the corners of her eyes.

"You promised," she said, her voice cracking.

Vox picked up the towel. "I have no intention of hurting you, nor will I force myself on you. But only if you keep your promise to me."

She flinched as he began rubbing the towel down her arms, relaxing slightly when she realized he was only drying her.

He patted her soaking hair, leaning closer until his face was inches from hers. "You should be glad it was me that took you, and not one of my Kronock crew mates. They would have already impaled you on their scaly cocks."

She made a strangled noise in the back of her throat as he bent lower to dry her legs, and she could feel warm puffs of his breath against her stomach. He dragged the towel between her legs, and she twitched from the touch.

"Lift your foot."

She looked down. "What?"

He crouched in front of her, the dress bunched near her feet. She lifted one foot and then the other so he could slip the dress over her legs. Leaning her head back and keeping her eyes closed, she felt the soft fabric pass over her knees and hips. He pulled it up over her stomach and her breasts, then tied the straps at the top of her shoulders.

Shreya opened her eyes and saw him appraising her, his gaze traveling from her feet up. When he reached her eyes, he closed the short distance between them and put a hand gently on her waist, his thumb rubbing up and down through the silky fabric. "Was that so bad?"

Her breath was quick and shallow as she shook her head, and a rush of heat throbbed between her legs. "Can you untie me now?"

"Soon enough." He traced a finger down her throat, leaning his face close and inhaling deeply. "You smell good enough to eat."

Shreya closed her eyes as he licked the side of her neck, her nipples pebbling and an unwanted shiver of pleasure jolting her body. *You do not want this*, she told herself. *You do not want him.*

Too bad her body hadn't gotten the message. As he made a low noise, shivers shot down her spine, and she fought to keep from moaning aloud. It was a good thing her hands were bound and holding her up, or she certainly would have collapsed.

His touch was almost gentle as his hands skimmed the front of her dress, brushing over her hard nipples, grazing her hips and caressing her thighs. When one hand dipped under the hem of her dress, her eyes snapped open and her legs clamped together.

Vox's face was above hers, and his one real eye peered down at her intensely. With one hand he held her hip, as he ran the other hand up her bare thigh. When he reached the place where her legs met, he paused.

"You're wet," he said, his fingers touching the slickness between her upper thighs. The pupil in his eye widened, the sea-green being overtaken by black.

Shreya pressed her lips together almost as tightly as she'd clamped her legs. What was wrong with her? Why was she getting turned on by this guy? Part-cyborg aliens definitely weren't her type, even if he was built. And she wasn't into bondage or kinky stuff, was she? Her pussy throbbed, and she cursed her traitorous body.

She closed her eyes again, bracing herself for him to force her legs open. Her body trembled and her breath was shallow. When she felt him pull away, her eyes flew open. Without a word, he dropped her dress and unstrapped her hands.

Rubbing her wrists, she stumbled away from him, even though she was unhurt. Shaken and freaked out by the fact that she'd gotten so aroused, yes, but not hurt.

"I told you I will wait until you ask me to claim you," he said, crossing to the table filled with bottles.

That would never happen, she told herself, trying to ignore the slickness between her thighs.

Chapter Six

Shreya watched him standing at the drinks cart. She wouldn't mind if he drank himself into oblivion, although considering his size, she didn't know if there was enough liquor on the table for that. From what she'd seen and heard, Drexians could handle their booze, and, despite his current identity crisis, his biology was still mostly Drexian. At least she thought it was.

She felt ridiculous in the flimsy dress and kept her arms crossed over her breasts, since the fabric provided little coverage. She shifted from one leg to the other and stared at her empty glass on the table. Although she rarely drank, she wouldn't have minded some more of whatever sweet drink he'd poured her. Anything to keep from dwelling on the deal she'd made, what she was wearing, and how her own body had reacted. What had she been thinking to agree to let him touch her? A shiver passed through her body, and she wasn't sure if it was wholly from fear.

It wasn't as if she'd had a choice, she told herself. Her other option had been to let him drag her off to bed right then and there. She believed him when he said no one would respond to her cries for help. It was clear he'd brought her to a place where women's screams were commonplace, and she suspected the winged madam was paid handsomely to look the other way.

"Bitch," she whispered to herself, as she thought about the alien fairy. She usually didn't like to trash other women, but in this case, she thought it was well-deserved. A female who made her living off the pain and imprisonment of other women was pretty low in Shreya's book, even if she did flit around on iridescent wings.

She didn't blame the little one, Cerise, who had shown them to the room. That creature had seemed as frightened as she was, and Shreya wondered what horrors she'd endured, living on this lawless planet.

Keeping one eye on Vox, she backed away until she reached a pair of chairs to one side of the bed. Even though she was exhausted, she didn't dare lie down. Instead, she sank into one of the plush, velvet chairs, letting herself relax against the gold-tufted pillows as she watched her captor from across the room.

Vox rubbed his forehead, leaning one hand against the table as his face contorted in obvious pain. She wondered if this had anything to do with what she'd discovered during her research. In decrypting the Kronock records, she'd learned that even though Kronock DNA had been added to his existing Drexian DNA, his cells had eventually begun to reject it.

Since she'd never seen the kind of experiments the Kronock had done on him, she had no idea what kind of reaction Vox's body would have when the Kronock DNA fully degraded. The reason she'd been on the rescue mission in the first place, had been so she could stabilize his DNA once they'd captured him. She'd prepared a series of injections she'd hoped would boost the Drexian DNA and stabilize it once the Kronock DNA broke down. Of course, all of that was back on the Drexian ship he'd abducted her from, which was probably light years from where she was now.

Shreya eyed him as he massaged his temples, his forehead creased as he grimaced in pain. If the DNA breakdown was happening faster than she'd anticipated, maybe she didn't have to worry about her promise. From the looks of it, the guy wouldn't be capable of doing much within a day or two. Maybe if she could wait him out, he'd keel over and she could escape.

Nice, she thought. Your entire mission was to save him and now you're going to wait until he dies?

Vox poured himself another drink, swirling the green liquid in the glass before slamming it back.

But she didn't really have a choice, did she? It wasn't like she had a lab, or any of her supplies. Even if she wanted to save the guy whose entire mission in life seemed to be to impregnate her, she didn't have the equipment to pull it off.

Vox pulled the scaly, gray armor over his head and set it on an upholstered bench. Beneath the armor, his chest was bare and huge.

Shreya couldn't help staring at him, her pulse quivering. Although his arms were partially scaled, the sculpted curves of his muscles looked smooth. Hard and sleek, she thought, as her gaze traveled lower, to the bumpy ridges of his stomach and the v-cut that disappeared beneath the waistband of his pants.

She jerked her gaze away, hoping he hadn't noticed her gaping. She also hoped that his stripping down wasn't a sign that he was ready to take her up on their deal. She swallowed, but her throat was dry, and she ended up coughing so hard she finally put her head between her knees.

"Drink this."

His voice jarred her, and she jumped when she realized he'd closed the distance between them and stood in front of her.

"Thanks." She took the drink, grateful for both the cool liquid to stop her coughing and for something to fill her stomach.

When she drained the glass, he took it from her, then took her other hand and pulled her up and started walking toward the bed.

"What are you…?" Her voice sounded high and shaky as she tried to pull away from him.

His gaze slid to the large bed. So much for him being too damaged. The booze must have given him liquid courage, or a boost of energy. After her body's recent reaction to him, she did not trust herself on a bed.

"You haven't told me anything about yourself," she said, her words coming out in a desperate tumble.

"What do you mean?"

"On Earth, people get to know each other first," Shreya said, pulling him to a stop. "We talk."

"Talk?" Vox tilted his head at her.

She nodded. "Always. You tell me things about you, and I tell you things about me."

"You do this before the…floor play?"

If she wasn't so terrified, she would have laughed. "Foreplay. Yes, on Earth we always get to know each other before there's any touching." Not always, she thought, but he didn't need to know that.

His bionic eye flashed. "Will it make you more willing if we get to know each other?"

"Definitely," she lied, knowing that no amount of talking would make her do something she didn't want to do. The real question was, what did her body want her to do?

"Okay." He released her hand. "I am Vox, and I am a member of the Kronock empire."

She walked back to the chair. "Is that your Kronock name?"

His head jerked, but he followed her, taking the chair next to hers. "No. It was from before."

Interesting, Shreya thought. He kept his Drexian name. She wondered if that had been his choice, or the Kronock's. "When you were Drexian?"

He nodded, his lips a firm line.

"How did you happen to join the Kronock?" she asked.

The red light in his cybernetic eye blinked faster. "I was in military intelligence, and was sent deep into Kronock territory to assess the danger."

"You were captured?"

His head jerked again and his speech became more stilted. "I was liberated by General Krav, and became a member of the glorious Kronock empire. Now I exist to carry out his final mission."

Shreya gulped, knowing his final mission was her.

He focused his green eye on her, leaning forward with his elbows on his knees. "Now it is my turn. Tell me why you are not a tribute bride."

Anything to keep him talking. "I guess it just wasn't my thing, marrying a total stranger and having alien babies."

"You do not wish to have offspring?"

"It's not my first priority," she said, pulling her bare feet up under herself. "I was still in college—being educated—when I was taken from Earth. I was focused on my degree and career more than anything else. I guess I didn't give kids much thought."

"And now?"

"Since I'm what we like to call an 'independent' on the Drexian station, it hasn't been an issue."

He moved to the edge of the chair. "You have not mated with any Drexians?"

"No." She shook her head firmly. "We aren't encouraged to fraternize with the warriors. You can ask my friend Ella about that."

"Then you have never…?" His gaze moved down her body.

"Oh, I have, but only with one guy," she admitted. "I honestly don't know what all the fuss is about. It wasn't all that great."

"How long ago was this 'not so great' guy?" Vox asked.

This was getting weird, Shreya thought. "Why do you care?"

He shifted. "I need to know there is no chance you are already carrying another warrior's seed."

She wrinkled her nose. "How romantic. First of all, he wasn't a warrior. He was a neurobiology grad student. And I'm definitely not 'carrying his seed.'" She made air quotes. "It was way before I was taken off Earth."

"Good." He stood and pulled her up. "That is enough talking for now."

If he thought that was enough talking, then he wasn't so different from human men, after all. Her heart hammered in her chest as he pulled her toward the bed, but before they reached it, there was a sharp rap on the door.

Vox stopped, and sighed before crossing to the door and opening it. The tiny woman from earlier pushed a wheeled cart into the room, her pink hair barely bobbing above the top. The clear cart was laden with plates of food and tiered towers of shimmering confections, the scent of both savory and sweet filling the air, and making Shreya's stomach growl.

"Compliments of the house," Cerise said in a cheery voice, seemingly unfazed by the fact that Vox was half-naked. She gave Shreya a sly wink once she'd passed him.

Shreya smiled back as relief flooded her body. Unless she was mistaken, Cerise had interrupted on purpose. As Shreya looked at the creature's mischievous expression, she wondered how easy it would be to convince Cerise to help her escape.

Chapter Seven

Vox felt a flash of irritation as he watched the Perogling wheel the food into the room. Had he requested it when he'd arranged things? Maybe, but he didn't remember. His memories were becoming muddled as the pains in his head grew more frequent.

The pink-haired creature pushed the cart toward the sitting area between the door and the bed, unloading the food onto the gilt-legged coffee table as she hummed. "Madam sent up food she thought a human might like."

Shreya came to stand by the small alien in the belled-out gown. "It smells wonderful."

"I hope you like it." The Perogling peered up at Shreya. "We've never had one of your kind here before, so I wasn't sure what you might like."

Vox cleared his throat and strode over to the women. Had a look just passed between them? It wasn't possible that they knew each other, but he could have sworn the little one had winked at his mate. "That's enough for now, Perogling. You may go."

The creature dipped into a curtsy before backing the now-empty cart out of the room. Vox watched her go with her head lowered. She did not make eye contact with Shreya again, closing the door behind her without looking up. He must have imagined the look between them. There was no way a human could know anyone on Lymora III, much less an alien pleasurer in the most notorious and tightly controlled pleasure house on the planet.

"Are there Peroglings on the Boat?" he asked, turning his attention back to the human.

Shreya glanced up, wiping stray sugar crystals off her lips. "Peroglings?"

Vox gestured at the door. "The alien who brought the food is a Perogling, a species of tiny creatures whose planet was destroyed millennia ago."

Shreya paused with a purple cream puff halfway to her mouth. "Her planet was destroyed?"

"Enough of her species escaped or were off-planet so her kind survived, but they were scattered throughout the galaxy. Many were sold into slavery, as the females are highly prized as pleasurers. I'm sure that is how this one ended up in the most exclusive pleasure house on Lymora III."

Shreya dropped the purple puff. "She's a slave?"

"I do not know for sure," he said, watching as the human's skin paled. "Most females here are paying off their debt to Zylia."

"Do they ever get free?"

"If they do, I doubt they would leave. Here they are safe and protected."

"But not free," Shreya said, her eyes narrowed.

"So you have never seen one of her kind before?" Vox asked, ignoring her pointed look.

She shook her head. "As far as I know, there aren't any… Peroglings on the Boat."

He picked up the puff she'd discarded. "Is this not good?"

She turned away. "I lost my appetite."

Vox scanned the table, inspecting the food and finding no traditional Kronock dishes, not that he'd ever grown used to Kronock food. Even as his body had become more Kronock and his mind had learned to regurgitate Kronock words, his taste buds had never adapted to the bitter, earthy flavors favored by the scaled race. He also saw little Drexian food, and tried to push aside his craving for cheedi berries. The only thing that looked familiar was a few pieces of fried padwump on a small plate, so he picked one up and took a bite.

"How do you know so much about this place?" Shreya asked.

He glanced up and saw that her arms were folded tightly across her chest. "From before."

"When you were a Drex—?"

"Yes." He cut her off as a pain shot through his implant. "I came here to gather intelligence and learned that Zylia had a price. Her girls see and hear a great deal from the aliens who pass through the house, and that information is always for sale."

"The fairy madam is a spy?"

Vox touched a hand to one throbbing temple. "Not a loyal one."

"So you didn't come here to…?"

"Sample the pleasures?" He finished her sentence for her, as he swallowed a bite of salty padwump. "I have been to pleasure houses before, but my visits here were always business. Drexians do not come here, because it is lawless and corrupt, and Kronock do not come here, because they do not need pleasure planets."

"Why not?"

He could hear the words in his head before he repeated them. "Kronock are superior. We do not to procreate organically anymore. It is done in the lab to create superior beings."

"So what are you doing here with me?"

"The lab cannot do everything." He did not meet her eyes. "This mission is different, and it is crucial to Krav's plan to invade Earth and destroy the enemy."

"You mean the Drexians?" she asked, her voice quavering. "Destroy the Drexians?"

Another pain and his head jerked. "I must fulfill Krav's mission." He finally looked up at her face, which was flushed pink. "You should eat."

She shook her head.

"I can force you to eat," he said.

Her eyes flared and she stomped over to the table, snatching up a brown, flaky ball and taking a bite. "Happy?"

"Why would that make me happy? I am glad you will not be weak from hunger, but Kronock do not get happy."

She rolled her eyes and flopped onto one of the nearby chairs. "Yeah, well, you're not going to be Kronock for long."

Vox did not ask what she meant, since he did not understand much of what the human said. He finished the padwump, but did not try another, as the traditional Drexian food tasted bitter to him now. Picking up a white, stick-shaped item, he took a bite. It was crunchy and cold, sending a burst of sweet juice down his throat.

He jumped a bit, surprised that the food had exploded in his mouth.

He looked up when he heard Shreya giggle and saw her holding a hand over her mouth and fighting to keep her scowl in place.

"The same thing happened to me when I tried that," she said, dropping her hand and relaxing her face.

He frowned and dropped it. "Very strange."

"If you think that's weird, it's a good thing you've never had Pop Rocks."

"Pop Rocks?" He tilted his head at her. "They sound dangerous. Is this an Earth weapon?"

She laughed again. "An Earth candy. They're supposed to be fun. Little colorful pebbles that pop and sizzle when you put them in your mouth."

He stared at her. "Humans find this fun?"

"Yeah, I guess we do."

Vox shook his head. "I remember hearing that Earthlings are fond of sugar. Is everything you eat on your planet sweet?"

"Not everything," Shreya said, standing and walking to the table. "But we do eat a lot of sugar, especially compared to Drexians. I don't think you guys even have dessert."

"Dessert?"

Shreya gestured to the tiered stand filled with colorful confections glistening with sugar crystals and dusted with copious amounts of powdered sugar. "Something sweet you eat at the end of every meal."

Vox bent closer to the sweets and inhaled. "Every meal?"

Shreya picked up an orange, diamond-shaped sweet dotted with gold flecks. "Try it before you knock it. This isn't as good as gulab jamun, but it's not bad."

Vox took it from her gingerly and nibbled the edge. Even from the small bite, he got a burst of flavor that reminded him faintly of cheedi berries. He took another bite, enjoying both the sweetness and the comfort of familiarity.

"See?" Shreya said. "Not bad, right?"

"Not bad," he admitted, sitting down on one of the upholstered chairs and jerking his head toward the table. "You should eat, and more than just…" he hesitated as he searched for the word, "dessert."

She picked up one of the exploding white sticks, using it to point at his face. "You have some gold stuff on you."

"Gold stuff?" He touched his fingers to his cheek.

She gave a shake of her head. "Lower. Near your lips."

Dropping his hand, he rubbed his mouth.

"Still no." She hesitated, then walked over and swiped a finger across his lower lip.

He caught her wrist before she could pull it back, holding her hand out and inspecting the flake of gold she'd wiped off his face. "Is this gold bad to eat?"

"No." She tried to tug her hand away. "I'm sure it's edible."

He put her finger in his mouth and sucked the gold off, hearing her gasp and feeling her hand go stiff. "You are right. It does not taste bad."

"Can you let me go?"

He noticed that a vein on the side of her neck pulsed. He glanced down at her finger. "Maybe what I liked tasting was not the gold. Maybe what tasted so good was you."

She made a small noise as he put her finger back in his mouth, savoring both the softness of her skin and the sound of her rapid breathing. He held tight as she tried to wrench her hand away from him, her struggle making his cock twitch. His gaze drifted to the swell of her breasts so evident through the fabric of the dress.

He knew he'd promised not to force her, but he found her resistance arousing. Even tasting such a small part of her—the soft tip of one finger—made him want more, and her futile movements to get away from him made Vox want to feel her entire body struggling beneath him.

He felt a surge of desire followed by a bolt of pain in his cybernetic eye so sharp it made him drop her wrist and clutch his implant. He heard her move away from him, her footsteps heading toward the entry.

As the pain subsided, he glanced over to where she stood at the handleless door, running her palms over the surface. "It is biometrically linked to me. You cannot open it, no matter how hard you try."

He stood and crossed to her as she sagged against the door, taking her by the hand. "Bed."

She pulled back as he walked toward the large bed, clawing at his arm. "You promised you wouldn't…."

His head ached, and he did not have time for this. He reached the bed and tossed her on it, watching her bounce and then scuttle toward the back. Vox reached up and found the straps above the bed. Pulling one strap taut, he grabbed for one of her arms.

She kicked out at him, screaming about him being a wanker, as he pulled one wrist toward him and strapped it down.

He dodged another hard kick as he clasped her other wrist and quickly fastened the fabric strap around it. She was now lying face up on the bed, her hands tied down over her head as she pulled against them.

Straddling her waist, he put a hand over her mouth to stop her screams. Her eyes were wild and she moved her head violently, trying to bite him.

"I have no intention of taking you right now, human," he said, his voice loud and echoing through the room. She stopped struggling, and he let out a breath. "I mean, Shreya."

She blinked up at him, and he slowly removed his hand from her mouth. Her dark hair spilled across the sheets and her face, and her cheeks flamed pink. If he didn't need to rest so badly, it would have been difficult not to touch her while she was tied up. The thought of running his fingers over the bare skin exposed by the low-cut dress was intoxicating, but he pushed the thought from his pounding head.

He smoothed a strand of hair off her forehead. "I need to sleep, and I can't have you trying to kill me while I do." Moving off her, he rolled onto his back, hearing nothing but her ragged breath as sleep overtook him.

Chapter Eight

"So I'm supposed to lie here with my hands strapped to the bed while you sleep?" Shreya asked, when she'd finally found her voice.

The only answer was the sound of rhythmic snoring. Had he actually fallen asleep so quickly?

Great. Just great. She tugged at the restraints, but they held fast. She hadn't held out much hope, since the straps looked like they'd been made for the express purpose of tying someone up. Black and padded around her wrists, the straps were thick and heavy duty. No silk scarves here. She arched her head back to see where they originated from and spotted a heavy, metal bolt on the wall. No surprise there. She guessed restraints weren't an unusual request in a place like this.

Sagging back down on the bed, Shreya let her arms relax. At least he hadn't tried anything yet. Not anything too terrifying. She supposed she should be glad about that. She twisted her neck so she could get a better look at the sleeping giant, a shudder passing through her as she studied his altered face.

The gray scales that grew on his arms had not extended to his face, which still looked very Drexian. At least half of it, anyway. Bronze skin, a square jaw, and only the slightest trace of stubble on his cheeks reminded her of the other warriors she'd grown accustomed to seeing on the space station. Until he rolled over, and she got a closeup of the metal implant that curved from above one eye, around his temple, and to the middle of his cheek. The cybernetic implant covered his eye socket, and she wondered if the other eye was underneath, or if it had been removed and replaced with the flashing red one that now faced her.

Shreya looked away, the implant and blinking light making her cringe. Had it hurt when they'd attached that to him? Idiot, she told herself. Of course it had. Especially if they'd removed his real eye.

A lump formed in her throat, as she thought of the beautiful, sea-green eye being cut out of him. Shreya gave her head a sharp shake and blinked away tears. Was she actually feeling sorry for the hybrid cyborg who'd kidnapped her, and was planning to impregnate her? She knew she shouldn't, but then again, he hadn't always been a part Kronock, part cyborg creature. He'd been taken, as well, and clearly brainwashed, as well as physically altered. She'd seen the records of the experiments they'd done on him, and had a pretty good idea of what the barbaric alterations were gradually doing to him.

He rolled over again, so that her only view was of his Drexian side once more. Seeing his face like that—handsome and peacefully sleeping—made her feel a flood of sympathy for him. Before all this he'd been a Drexian, and she knew the Drexians valued honor and loyalty above all. Vox never would have done this if he hadn't been made into a monster by the Kronock. And now, he would die because of them, as his DNA degraded and his body collapsed.

She tightened her hands into fists over her head, understanding more and more why the Drexians were so hell-bent on defeating the Kronock, and feeling grateful they'd pledged to defend Earth from the violent aliens. She may not call the planet her home anymore, but she would be devastated to think of the Kronock getting their claws on it.

Vox mumbled in his sleep and thrashed his arms. Shreya rolled herself out of his way, knowing that having one of his huge, muscular arms land on her would hurt, even if it was accidental.

"Are you okay?" The soft whisper made her jerk around.

Cerise stood by the bed, her small stature placing her at eye level with Shreya. Her iridescent-blue skin had undertones of pink, and reminded Shreya of mother of pearl, the way it shifted color as it caught the light.

Shreya darted a glance at Vox before turning back to her. "Should you be here?"

"Probably not," Cerise said, her bright-pink bow of a mouth stretching into a smile. "But he should be out for a while." She jerked her head toward the food. "I saw he ate at least one piece."

Shreya followed her gaze. "One piece of what?"

"The only Drexian thing over there. Padwump. I thought he might be drawn to it. Even though he claims to be with the Kronock empire, I know a Drexian when I see one."

Shreya listened to Vox's deep breathing. "You drugged it?"

Cerise nodded and giggled.

"Thank you." Shreya's admiration for the tiny alien grew. She wiggled her arms. "Can you untie me?"

Cerise's face fell. "Untie you? No, not yet."

"What do you mean, not yet? Why did you drug him, if not to help me get out of here?"

Cerise glanced behind her at the door. "I needed to talk to you first."

Shreya tried not to snap at the woman, even though she wanted desperately to be free of the restraints. "Okay, what do you want to talk about?"

"You came to Lymora III on a ship, right? A private ship?"

"Yes, it was a private ship. Why?" Shreya snuck a peek at Vox, grateful he still slept soundly, but knowing that might not last for very long.

Cerise leaned closer. "Can you fly it?"

At that point, Shreya would have claimed to be able to do anything as long as the little alien would free her. "Pilot the ship? Sure, I can."

"Then we can escape, and you will take me with you," Cerise said.

"Absolutely. Untie me and we can get the hell off this planet." She was perfectly fine with bringing the woman with her. Actually, the thought of liberating a possible sex slave from the fairy madam gave her a bit of a rush. It would serve Zylia right for enslaving other women.

Cerise beamed. "Do you promise?"

"I give you my word," Shreya said, meaning it with every fiber of her being.

Vox grunted and shifted on his sleep.

Cerise jumped. "Now isn't the time, but I will return."

"Wait," Shreya whispered, as she watched the creature's ruffled skirt swing back and forth as she hurried toward the door. "You can't leave me like this."

Cerise's garishly-made-up face twisted into a frown as she paused at the door and turned around. "I'm sorry, but we can't give him any reason to suspect."

Shreya understood, but she still hated to be left so helpless. A single tear snaked down her cheek as Cerise pressed a palm to the large door, and it opened for her. Then she was gone.

Lying on the bed, she steadied her breathing as she listened to Vox's rhythmic exhales. Thankfully, he'd slept through everything. He had no idea there was a traitor in the bordello, or that he'd been drugged. Most importantly, he had no clue that Shreya now had someone who was going to help her escape.

She didn't know when Cerise would be back for her, but she knew she just needed to hold out until she did. Since Vox had given her his word that he wouldn't force her, all she needed to do was grit her teeth and get through anything he might try to weaken her defenses.

She wanted to think that would be easy, but she couldn't forget how her body had betrayed her earlier. Shreya hated to think she might be attracted to this part-cyborg alien, but she knew it was the Drexian part that made her pulse flutter. That, and the fact that she hadn't so much as touched a man in years.

She'd been honest when she'd told Vox that she'd only been with one guy, and it hadn't been anything to write home about. She honestly didn't get what the big fuss was about sex. In her experience, it was awkward, fumbling, and quick. Her one and only partner had been a nice guy, but she suspected he'd had about as much experience as she had. Each of their few encounters had lasted less than five minutes and had barely elevated her heart rate.

She'd have no problem resisting *that*, although there was something about Vox that made her worry. Shreya hoped it was a combination of nerves and fear that made her pulse quicken and her skin tingle when he touched her.

She tried to steady her heartbeat and relax. She needed to get rest if she was going to stage an escape. Closing her eyes, she was aware of the heat radiating off her captor's massive body as she drifted off to sleep.

Chapter Nine

Vox looked down at her, his head swimming. Why did he feel so groggy? He knew the day had been exhausting, but Shreya didn't look sleepy, even though she'd woken up right after him.

He closed his eyes, put a hand to his implant, and pressed on it. Was his cybernetic optical processor malfunctioning? That would explain the pains, and why he felt so tired. Unfortunately, there was nothing he could do about an issue with his implant. Until he returned to Kronock space, that was, and he had no intention of going back until he'd completed his mission.

He opened his eyes. The human female still stared up at him, her breathing almost silent, as if she was hoping she could be quiet enough that he wouldn't notice her.

Impossible, he thought. Not when she was so desirable. And completely at his mercy. General Krav's instructions rushed to the forefront of his mind, the sharp words echoing in his brain.

Females are to be dominated. They must submit.

He would like this pretty female to submit to him, but he would not take her as he knew Krav would have. He would not be rough and bruising, spreading her legs and forcing himself inside. That was not the way he wanted her. No, he wanted her to be willing.

Vox inhaled, breathing in the scent of her hair. He took a strand between his fingers and stroked it, hearing her draw a quick breath. Even though her hair was thick, it was deceptively silky. He imagined it falling across his bare skin, and heat flared in his core.

"You slept," he said. A statement, not a question.

She nodded without speaking.

"I thought you might be afraid to sleep next to me."

Her eyes narrowed slightly. "I'm not afraid of you."

"Good." He dropped her hair and traced a finger down her cheek, stopping at her mouth. "I will not hurt you."

Running his finger along the seam of her lips, he fought the urge to taste her. He wanted to crush his mouth to hers, but he knew it was too soon. He needed to go slow.

Vox scanned her body lying prone on the bed. He had so much to explore, and so many ways to arouse her. He may not have frequented this particular pleasure house, but he had the insatiable aliens of Tybor's notable houses of pleasure to thank for teaching him how to take his time.

Using only the tips of his fingers, he stroked the skin down her neck until he reached the gentle swell of her cleavage. He lowered his mouth and kissed softly between her breasts, feeling her heart pounding.

"Why don't we talk some more?" she said. "You know, get to know each other."

"I am getting to know you." Sitting back, he began untying the straps of her dress.

She jerked and pulled at her restraints. "What do you think you're doing?"

"Nothing you didn't agree to."

"Please stop."

The pleading tone of her voice gave him pause, and he stopped. "I thought we already got to know each other."

He already knew he desired her. What more did he need to know? Drexians were assigned human mates, and the Kronock reproduced artificially, so the entire concept seemed strange to him. He had to admit to being curious about her, however, so the idea of knowing more about the human did not repel him.

"Where did you grow up?" she asked, before he could resume undressing her.

Vox closed his eyes, the question bringing up hazy memories. "A colony on Ferngor. It's a planet with significant resources that my father helped defend from the…"

"What was it like?" Shreya asked, ignoring him stumbling over admitting that it was the Kronock his father had been defending against.

"Wet. The planet is mostly water, with thousands of islands linked together by bridges or underwater tunnels."

"We have one of those on Earth." Her face brightened. "The Chunnel. It goes between England and France. I've been in it a couple of times. Terrifying to be under so much water."

"I've never been afraid of water," Vox said, realizing this about himself as he said it, and recalling memories of himself swimming as a boy.

Shreya's expression clouded. "You've never been in a tsunami then."

"What is a soo-na-mi?" he asked, sounding out the curious word.

"A giant wave." Her gaze dropped, as did her voice. "So much water rushing in, you think it won't ever stop."

He watched her pull her knees up to curl into a ball. "You were in one of these tsunamis?"

A single nod. "My whole family was. I was the only one who made it out."

Even though Vox had been conditioned not to have emotional responses, his stomach tightened as he watched the female try not to cry. "Then you were lucky."

She laughed weakly. "Yeah, you can see how lucky I am. No offense, but being kidnapped and tied up by a part-cyborg alien isn't what I'd call winning the lottery."

He didn't know what that meant, but he flinched at her description of him as part cyborg. He touched the metal on his face. "Does my implant bother you?"

She flicked her eyes at it, then away just as quickly. "Not much. Does it hurt you?"

"Not much."

"What about when they put it in?" she asked.

His body jerked unconsciously at the memory. "That was painful, but Kronock can withstand a great deal of pain. Did your body augmentation hurt?"

She tilted her head at him. "My body augmentation?"

He touched her earlobes, and the small, gold earrings she wore.

"My pierced ears? No, that stung for about a second, but I was really young so I barely remember it."

"These pierced ears are only for ornamentation? No practical purpose?" he twisted the gold studs. "They are not transmitters?"

"I wish," she muttered. "No, it's just for ornamentation, as you call it. I know some of you guys do body ornamentation."

"Our implants are not for ornamentation."

"I meant tattoos," she said, her gaze moving to his bare chest. "I've seen some Drexians with some pretty serious tattoos."

"Inferno Force. They prefer markings. I never had them, since I was in military intelligence." He hesitated, momentarily startled that the information had flowed so freely from him. For a second, his mind had cleared, and he'd felt like his old self again. He'd felt Drexian. Then he heard General Krav's voice in his head, and what was left of his former self drifted away again.

Hearing the rough, guttural commands repeating in his mind made him frown. The human was distracting him from his mission. The past was irrelevant. There was only the future. A future where the Kronock had dominion over the galaxy. A future that depended on destroying the humans and the Drexians. A future that depended on Krav's plan. And her.

Vox leveled his gaze at Shreya. "That is enough 'getting to know each other'."

Her body stiffened, as he turned his attention to the ear he'd been absently touching. He leaned in, taking one lobe and sucking it while he finished untying the straps of her dress.

Shreya emitted a soft gasp, and her body jerked. Vox traced his tongue around her ear before sitting back and pulling down the top of the dress. His breath faltered when he saw the globes of her breasts, the warm brown of her skin begging him to touch it.

Her pupils darkened. "This isn't going to work, you know."

"What isn't going to work?" He dragged a finger along the soft skin, barely grazing her nipple, which hardened in response.

She drew in a jagged breath. "It doesn't matter what you do. I'm not going to want you."

His finger brushed her pebbled skin, and he noted her breath quickening. "I am not sure if your body agrees with you."

Chapter Ten

She closed her eyes and pressed her lips together, in an attempt to stop her body's response. *You do not want this,* she told herself. *You do not want him. Cyborg aliens with scales are not your type. You like nice, nerdy guys. Not huge, hunky aliens with split personalities.*

Blowing out a long breath, she gritted her teeth and tried to ignore the feel of his fingers on her skin. For such a massively muscled guy, his touch was surprisingly gentle.

"What if I asked you to stop?" she said, her eyes still tightly shut. "What if I told you I didn't like this?"

His breath was warm against her neck as he kissed the hollow of her throat, and she was unable to control the shiver of pleasure that passed through her body.

"I would not believe you," he whispered.

He kissed his way down her chest as she pulled at the restraints. Shreya desperately wanted to cover herself. Even the one guy she'd been with had never seen her like this, since they'd fooled around mostly in the dark. She didn't think he'd ever seen her undressed, which had been fine by her. She was usually embarrassed by the thought of being naked.

"You are perfect," he said, his moth reaching her breasts and capturing one nipple in his mouth.

Her eyes almost rolled up into the back of her head as he swirled his tongue around the hard nipple, and she fought the urge to arch her back so he could take more of her in his mouth.

What is wrong with you? You're supposed to be fighting against this, she told herself through the haze of desire clouding her brain's attempts at reason.

The sensations of his hot, wet mouth on her were almost too much to take. How did this hybrid alien know how to make her body respond the way he did? She fisted her hands over her head and tried to regain control, focusing her mind on anything but the gorgeous alien sucking her nipple.

When he switched to the other side and began flicking at her with the tip of his tongue, she gave up. She couldn't fight her body's traitorous response—the short breaths, the hot skin, the wetness between her legs. At this rate, she *would* be begging him to fuck her.

He cupped the breast that was not in his mouth, rolling the hard nipple between two fingers and matching the rhythm with that of his tongue. She pressed her legs together, feeling the tingle that shot through her body.

"Vox," she gasped, her words escaping between pants.

She knew she was close, although she didn't know how since he'd never shifted his attention from her breasts. Without slowing his pace, he pressed his free hand between her legs, his thumb rubbing her clit through the gauzy fabric. It was enough to send her careening off the edge.

Jerking against her restraints, Shreya cried out as she bucked up, her body convulsing as the sensations barreled through her, leaving her panting and limp.

Vox kissed her breasts softly before he sat back.

Her eyelids were heavy as she caught her breath. "I didn't know that was possible."

"Many things are possible," he said. "Would you like me to show you more?"

She bit the edge of her bottom lip. "I don't think that's a good idea."

He nodded as if he agreed with her, while he shimmied the fabric up her thighs. "You sure you want me to stop?"

Instead of answering, she let out a small, breathy sigh. She knew she *should* want him to stop, but it was hard to think clearly with so many endorphins careening through her body. Her scientist mind tried to remind her that it was all chemical. She didn't feel anything for the alien who'd made her come just from sucking her nipples. It was the endorphins she was into. Not him.

Before he pushed the dress up to the top of her thighs, a voice made her jump. It was not his, but came from his implant.

"Vox of Kronock. Status update." The Kronock voice was guttural and sharp, making him flinch as well.

That broke the spell. She tried to sit up, imagining hordes of the scaly aliens breaking through the door.

Vox got off the bed and strode to the other side of the room.

"Vox of Kronock here."

"Status update," the faceless Kronock voice repeated.

"En route," he said, glancing back at her and lowering his voice. "After a delay that was unavoidable."

"You should have arrived at the lab by now, but we see you've stopped on Lymora III."

"Yes," Vox said. "Slight ship malfunction. I will be departing soon."

"Make sure you do. You are overdue for an injection."

"What?" Vox rubbed his temple. "What type of injection? Does this have anything to do with the pains in my head?"

A long pause from the Kronock. "Affirmative."

"Will they get worse if I'm delayed?"

"A delay would be inadvisable."

"So that's a yes," Vox muttered.

"Proceed to the Kronock lab as soon as possible or we will retrieve you for your own safety."

Vox released a breath. "Understood. Vox out." He turned back to the bed.

"Who were you talking to?" she asked, although she'd heard the conversation pretty clearly.

"No one." He shook his head, instinctively touching his implant. "It isn't important."

"Do you get messages through that thing? Can they track you through the implant in your head?"

"I disabled my internal tracker, but they clearly tracked my ship." He frowned. "I am too valuable to lose, but they will not come after me. Not yet. For now, they trust me to follow orders."

"And will you?" Shreya asked. "Follow their orders?"

He took long steps to the bed. "It depends on how well you follow mine."

Chapter Eleven

Before he reached the bed, a pain tore through his head, and he staggered against a chair. He heard Shreya scream as his hand slipped from the back of the chair, and he crashed to the floor.

There was another jolt of pain, but he didn't know if it was from his impact with the floor or his ocular implant. He was vaguely aware of a high voice calling his name, as he fought off the blackness that threatened to engulf him.

He had to stay conscious. He'd been telling the truth when he'd told her no one would respond to her screams. In a place like this, she could scream for help for hours and no one would raise an eyebrow. Which meant he could teeter on the brink of death with no help coming if he didn't get up.

When he'd finally crawled from the floor to the chair and staggered over to the bed, Shreya's eyes were wild.

"If you don't untie me right now so I can help you, I'm going to bite my way through these things," she said, her voice barely suppressing her fury.

He didn't argue, unstrapping her before sinking onto the bed. Vox was only slightly aware of her dressing and leaving the bed, but he was in too much pain to reach for her and pull her back.

"Here." She jabbed something cold and hard at his hand. "At least this should numb the pain."

He opened his eyes to see her holding a glass of whiskey, the green liquid filled almost all the way to the rim of the squat glass. Pushing himself up onto one elbow, he took the glass and sipped it slowly.

"Don't worry," she said as she watched him drink. "I didn't poison it."

He hesitated with the glass at his lips. It had never occurred to him she would poison him. "Thank you, I think."

She folded her arms over her chest. "Listen. We need to make another deal. You can't keep tying me up if you're going to pass out and almost kill yourself. I do *not* want to starve to death strapped to a bed just because you're paranoid I'm going to murder you in your sleep."

"What do you suggest?" He swallowed a mouthful of whiskey, grateful that it burned his throat and made him feel more alert.

"I'll promise not to murder you if you stop with the bondage thing."

General Krav's voice thundered in his head with warnings. *Do not trust her. Make her submit.*

He shook his head. He could not successfully complete his mission if he collapsed and she was unable to help him.

"No?" her voice brought him back to reality. "You don't agree?"

He focused on her face, her eyes unblinking. "I apologize. I was thinking of something else. Yes, I agree to your terms. You will not murder me, and I will not tie you up while I sleep."

"At all," she corrected. "You won't tie me up at all."

He sighed, too weak to argue further. "Fine."

She touched her fingers to his forehead. "Did you hurt yourself when you fell? I don't see any blood, but you might have a lump."

He raised his hand to cover hers, the heat of her skin comforting. "Your pulse is still fast."

She pulled away. "Well, I did see you collapse while I was barbarically strapped to a bed. And that was after you took advantage of me."

He cocked his head at her. "I do not remember you complaining when I was sucking you."

Her cheeks flamed red.

He wanted to touch them and see if they felt as hot as they looked, but his arms still felt sluggish. "Does it bother you to talk about being pleasured?"

She jutted her chin up. "No, but I'm not used to hearing someone talk about it like that."

"Like what?" He did not understand humans very well.

"I don't know," she said. "Like it's no big deal."

He drained the rest of his whiskey. "I think it will be a very big deal when I claim you as mine."

She jerked away. "And all this talk about claiming and mates is so dramatic. The way you guys talk about it, it's like medieval meets cave man."

"I do not know what either of those things mean, but claiming a mate for life is a big deal. When I take you, you will be mine. No other Drex...no one else will be able to claim you."

"I thought the Kronock were in charge of this whole 'plan'." She

65

made gestures in the air with her fingers. "You think they're going to play by the Drexian honor system?"

Her words were like barbs, awakening his own fears. Even though he was now Kronock, he knew he would never be free to take her as a mate the way he would have before. Before. He cringed at the word, trying not to think of life before he'd been taken and changed. There was no point. They'd made him into one of them and even implanted him with one of their devices. They could reach him anywhere, their words piercing his brain no matter how far he ran. He knew what they could do to him if he resisted. The Kronock had no problem delivering pain, and he'd been on the receiving end of much of it.

"They will not touch you if you are mine," he said, although the promise was hollow to his ears.

He knew she was right. The Kronock would take what they needed. They had taken him and they would take her, no matter how much it hurt, or how much she begged for them to stop. He squeezed his eyes shut to stop the memories of his own screams.

"I don't belong to anyone," she said, her voice soft but steady.

"If they take you, you will wish you belonged to me."

Vox watched her recoil, then stand and cross to the bed, sitting on the edge with her back to him. He felt the familiar tug within himself as voices echoed through his head, at war with his instincts. He knew he couldn't take her anywhere near the Kronock. Not if he wanted to keep her for himself. But if they were right and he needed treatment, then he might not last long enough to fulfill his mission. At least not the way he wanted to.

His gaze went to Shreya—her hair dark spilling down the low-cut back of her dress. His instincts rose up and overtook the Kronock programming. He would not let them touch her. She was his, only his, and he would die before he let them lay one clawed hand on her perfect body.

Chapter Twelve

She had to get out of there. Shreya peeked over her shoulder at Vox and shuddered. It wasn't even the thought of him that scared her anymore; it was the idea of the Kronock. He was delusional if he thought they wouldn't show up and demand he turn her over. Or insist that he mate with her right then and there. She suspected the scaly creatures would have little use for their deal or even for the concept of foreplay.

She didn't know what Cerise's timeline was, but she needed to move it up in a serious way. At least she'd gotten Vox to agree not to tie her up, but he seemed obsessed with the idea of claiming her and making her his mate. It seemed like the Kronock hadn't been able to brainwash all the Drexian instincts out of him, after all.

Shreya hadn't rejected being a tribute bride and gone to live in the low-rent section of the Boat just to be forced to be someone's mate. Not that she thought for a minute the Kronock would allow Vox to keep a mate in the traditional way, and the idea of being used for whatever sadistic plan they'd cooked up to bring down the Drexians and Earth was not appealing.

As much as he vowed to protect her, she knew Vox was still under

Kronock control. The glimpses she got of his former Drexian self didn't mean he wouldn't be forced to do what they wanted him to in the end. They could literally transmit commands through his cybernetic implant, she thought with a disgusted shake of her head.

Escaping was her best option, and Cerise was her ticket out of the bordello and back to the ship. If she could just get a message to her.

She thought for a minute, then turned around. "I have an idea."

Vox looked up. The way his head was turned, and the implant obscured, he looked completely Drexian.

Shreya continued without waiting for his response. "It's a game."

He looked confused. "A game? Why would I want to play a game?"

"I don't know." She opened her arms wide. "Maybe because there's nothing else to do in here."

"There are many things we can do."

Her throat felt dry. She knew exactly the things he meant, her eyes drifting to the contraption hanging in the corner. "This will be more fun."

"I doubt that."

She ignored him. "I need some supplies. Can you call for Cer—for the little alien who delivered the food?"

He eyed her with suspicion. "You will not ask her for a blade or a blaster?"

Shreya rolled her eyes at him. "Do you think anyone in this place would bring me either of those, since they know I'm your captive?"

"No, I do not think they would." He stood and walked to the door, opening it and leaning out.

After a few moments, the tiny alien entered the room, her pink bouffant bobbing as she walked. "You needed something?"

Shreya jumped off the bed. "Yes, we need supplies for a game."

Cerise's lavender, arched brows lifted as she produced an electronic tablet from a fold deep within her ruffled dress.

Shreya took it from her. "Here. Let me write it down." She paused with her finger on the screen. "Will you be able to translate it?"

Cerise exchanged a quick look with Vox that told Shreya her question had been silly. "Of course."

She finished her list and handed it back to the woman. "If you can't source all of it, don't worry."

Cerise swiped the screen a few times, the corners of her mouth twitching up for a beat then her expression becoming blank again. "I will be back very soon, miss."

When she'd left, closing the door behind her, Vox folded his arms across his chest. "There is no point to this."

"Of course there is. It's something to distract me from the fact that I'm being held in a weird bondage room and to distract you from the pains in your head. Plus, I'm hungry."

"Hungry? This game involves food?" He scanned the picked-over plates on the table. "We have food."

"Different food." She grinned. "Fun food."

Vox wrinkled his brow.

"Come on," Shreya said. "Didn't you play games when you were a kid?"

"We played many water games, but none involving food."

Actually, Shreya had never played food games as a child, either, but this was the fastest way she could think of to get a message to

Cerise and to get Vox out of the way. She'd already seen that Cerise was skilled at drugging food. If Shreya could convince Vox to eat a larger amount this time, he should be down for the count. He'd woken up too quickly the last time, and she knew they'd need a serious head start to get through the city and to the ship.

She hadn't worked out all the details of her new food game, but she suspected that he'd go along with it if she made it a little kinky. A guy who requested a room decked out with restraints would probably be up for that.

There was a knock on the door before Cerise entered again, rolling another multilevel cart. Shreya hurried over to her, inspecting what was beneath the shiny domes and nodding with approval.

"Thank you," she told the alien. "This looks great. Now all we need is a blindfold."

Cerise reached into the ruffled mass of her dress, producing a black blindfold with a flourish.

Shreya's eyebrows shot up, but Cerise only shrugged. "All the girls here carry one. And a whip. Do you need one of those?"

"No," Shreya said quickly, taking the blindfold. "Definitely no whips."

Cerise shrugged again, rolling the cart over to the table and switching out the used dishes for the new ones. Vox walked over and tried to lift one of the domes off a plate.

Shreya swatted at his hand. "Oh, no you don't. You'll spoil the game." She caught Cerise's eye and gave her a pointed look. "I don't want it to be over in five minutes."

"Minutes?" Cerise giggled. "How many beats are in a minute?"

"Beats?" Shreya looked at Vox.

"Heartbeats," he said, touching his bare chest. "On Lymora III, they measure time in standard heartbeats."

Shreya put a hand to her own heart. "I guess a minute is about sixty heartbeats."

Cerise's face lit up. "So a minute is a thrum."

"Okay," Shreya said. "Then I don't want the game to be over in five thrums."

Cerise nodded and finished loading the dirty plates, touching one finger on the top of a shiny, gold dome as she passed her hand over it to put the last plate on the cart. "Will there be anything else?"

Shreya shook her head, making note of the dome the alien had touched. The drugs must be in whatever food was under there. Her pulse quickened, and her palms felt sweaty, as she watched the tiny woman leave again.

"Are you going to explain this?" Vox asked.

She jerked her head up. "What?"

"The game. Are you going to explain the game or should I just start eating."

Shreya steadied her breathing. He didn't suspect anything. He only wanted to move things along, since he was no doubt humoring her.

Be convincing, she told herself. Make him believe you.

Smiling as brightly as she could, even though her face felt like it was trembling, she led him by the hand to the bed, patting the edge. "Sit and let me blindfold you."

He narrowed his eyes at her. "How do I know you won't try to escape?"

She sighed and tried to sound exasperated. "I'm not tying you up.

Besides, the door is still locked. All you have to do is pull off the blindfold and grab me."

He circled one arm around her waist. "I could grab you now, and we could forget about this silly game."

She wagged a finger at him and tried to wiggle away. "Not yet. First, let's see how good you are at this."

He released his grip. "After your game, we will play mine."

She tried to ignore the dark purr of his voice. She knew exactly what his game entailed. Fastening the blindfold around his head, she returned to the table for the plate Cerise had indicated. Pulling off the dome, she saw that it was filled with fluffy cream.

Whipped cream, or at least the closest thing they had to whipped cream in this place. She suspected this wasn't the first time a guest had requested this.

She sat next to Vox with the plate in her lap. "The object of the game is for you to guess what I'm feeding you."

He grunted. "This does not sound like much of a game."

"That's because you haven't played yet." She scooped some cream onto the tip of her index finger. "Open wide."

He did as she was told, and she teased the edge of his lips with her finger before sliding the fluffy cream into his mouth. He moaned as he sucked the cream off, and she dragged her finger out.

"See?" She tried to keep her voice even as her own heart began to beat faster. "Isn't this a fun game?"

He made a move to remove his blindfold, but she caught his hand. "Not yet. You haven't guessed the food yet."

"I have never tasted anything like this before."

"Then you get another taste." She used two fingers this time, getting a bigger scoop in his mouth and pumping her fingers back and forth a few times before drawing them out. She'd only used about half the mound of airy cream on the plate. She didn't know how potent it was, but he was a big guy, so she wanted to use all of it.

His moan became a growl. "I think it is time for my game."

"Not yet," she said, hearing the desperate tone of her voice and modulating it. "One more special taste and then you can give up."

She looked down at the remaining pile of white fluff. Unless she tried to pour it down his throat, which she doubted he'd go for, there was only one way to get him to eat all of it before he lost patience with her.

Here goes nothing, she thought, untying one side of her dress. She smeared the rest of the cream on her breast, her nipple hardening into a tight point as it was hit with the cold, wet fluff.

Standing so her breast was at his eye level, she took a deep breath and moved closer so that her nipple brushed his lips. Almost instantly, he sucked in a quick breath, pulling her closer. Vox groaned as he started to suck the whipped cream off her nipple, swallowing and taking her deep into his mouth.

Her hands went to his hair, clutching it as her knees almost buck-led. She knew this was all part of her game, and that her game was to get away from him, but his mouth felt so good on her that she almost forgot the objective. Her head fell back as ripples of plea-sure rocketed through her.

"I forfeit the game," he murmured when he pulled his mouth off her for a moment, then licked the stray bits of cream that he'd missed.

With the blindfold covering his cybernetic eye, she could almost imagine he was a normal man, and she ran a hand down the smooth side of his face. "I'm sorry."

He pulled off the blindfold and gazed up at her, his one real pupil constricting as she watched. "Do not be sorry. I like your game very much."

She leaned down and kissed him, tasting the bitter sweetness of the cream on his lips and in the back of her throat as his tongue swirled with hers. Then his lips went slack, and he slumped back on the bed. "I'm sorry for this, and sorry I can't save you."

Staggering back, Shreya tried to tie her dress back up, her fingers fumbling with the sheer fabric. She swiped at her lips, but she knew she'd ingested some of the cream. She'd barely managed to make a knot with the straps when the door swung open.

"Ready to fly?" Cerise asked, her brightly painted eyes unblinking.

Chapter Thirteen

G iving one final glance to the alien lying motionless on the bed, Shreya nodded. "Perfect timing."

Cerise stayed in the doorway, looking behind her and waving for Shreya to join her. "Come on. I gave some of your fluffed cream to the door guard, but I'm not sure how long until it wears off."

Shreya remembered how big the creature was who guarded the door, and she hurried across the room. Her head felt heavy—no doubt from the cream she'd accidentally eaten—but she couldn't let that slow her. "It will just knock them out, though. It won't kill them, right?"

The small alien beamed up at her, her bright smile never wavering. "I don't think it will kill them, but I don't do this often."

Shreya saw her shoes tucked in a corner near the door and slipped them on, then grabbed one of the brown cloaks she and Vox had arrived in.

"But you *have* done it before," Shreya said, more a statement than a question, since she got the feeling there was a lot more to Cerise than appearances would lead yone to believe.

The alien shrugged one shoulder, her smile flickering briefly. "Sometimes it's helpful for a client to sleep for a while."

Shreya thought the little woman had probably developed quite a few tricks to make life more bearable in a bordello on a brutal pleasure planet. "Thanks for helping me." She put a hand on the tiny alien's shoulder as the creature morphed into two versions of herself then went back to one. Great, she had double vision. She cursed the effects of the drugged cream, and hoped she hadn't swallowed too much.

Cerise's wide smile returned, and her voice dropped to a whisper. "Don't thank me yet. We still have to get downstairs without Zylia catching us."

Shreya's stomach tightened as she thought about the fairy madam, and she scanned the circular hallway that ringed the staircase that seemed to be moving on its own. "Is there a back exit?"

"Only through the sewers."

"Let's leave that as our back-up plan."

Cerise giggled, tiptoeing forward, her full skirt swaying silently as she walked, like a bell without a clapper. Shreya followed, also on her toes, holding her breath and lifting the long, draping fabric of her dress as they descended the spiraling stairs. Fear sharpened her mind and dampened the effect of the cream, but she still clutched the bannister tightly.

Light no longer streamed in from above, the towering foyer bathed in shadows instead of sunbeams. It must have been nighttime, although she suspected day and night meant little to the occupants of the pleasure house. Her room hadn't had windows, and she guessed most of the others didn't either, so guests would more easily lose track of time.

They passed several heavy doors much like the one to her suite, and occasionally, Shreya heard muffled noises from within that made her cheeks warm—moans of pleasure, screams of release, and the slapping of body against body. She jumped when she heard the crack of a whip, clamping a hand over her own mouth to keep from yelping in surprise.

Cerise turned and put a finger to her lips, giggling again. "A smuggling vessel arrived an hour ago, so most of the girls are busy."

Shreya wondered what kind of alien smugglers were behind the locked doors, but she also didn't want to find out. They hurried down the final curve of the stairs to reach the white-marble entrance hall where the massive, black-furred guard sat propped against the arched wall, his hooved feet flopped out and his tail tucked neatly in his lap. The creature breathed heavily, with his maned head lolling to one side.

Shreya's heart pounded so loudly she was sure it echoed through not only her own ears, but the airy foyer, and she couldn't help holding her breath as they edged around the guard. Cerise pointed to the narrow opening in the door propped open by a pair of tiny magenta shoes. Eyeing the slim space, Shreya almost told Cerise she couldn't fit through, but one more look at the sleeping giant made her determined to force her way through.

The small alien's ruffled skirts contracted as she turned sideways and slipped outside, a pink ruffle the last thing to disappear into the darkness. Sucking in a deep breath, Shreya followed. For once, she was grateful she didn't have large breasts, although even her C cups were flattened painfully as she squeezed her torso between the stone door and the frame. She tugged hard to get her ass and hips free, finally falling forward and almost landing on the stone walkway.

Shreya thought she heard the beating of wings as Cerise pulled the shoes from the gap in the door, and it closed behind them with a soft thud. The Perogling stepped into the miniature, buckle-up platform shoes, and instantly grew an extra inch. Giving a final, long look at the high, arched door, the alien jerked her head toward an alley that extended off the main path. "This way."

The two women ran down the close passageway, the buildings on either side not even an arm's length apart, their shoes pattering on the stone that occasionally gave way to dirt. Although it was dark, a trio of moons hung in the sky and weak light shone down, illuminating the ground enough for them to step over cracks and dodge bits of stray debris.

The spicy aroma of the pleasure house no longer filled Shreya's nose. Now it was the stench of rotten food, stale booze, and urine that made her put a hand over her mouth as they ran, fighting the urge to gag. Even on an alien world, neglect and debauchery carried the same smells.

They didn't sound so different, either. Despite the late hour, the faint, tinny notes of a horn drifted from an open window followed by a peal of laughter. Somewhere a bottle shattered and voices were raised. Behind them, someone stumbled out of a doorway, and shouted for them to stop and show him their tits.

Cerise never slowed, her pace impressive for one with such short legs, and soon, sweat beaded on Shreya's brow, in spite of the cool night air. After making several more turns and winding down even narrower passageways, Cerise stopped, one hand on her tiny waist as she drew in sharp breaths. "If Zylia is on our trail, I think we lost her."

Shreya instinctively glanced up at the night sky as she rested her hands on her knees. No beautiful yet terrifying fairy hovered above them, and she hoped the sound of wings she thought she'd heard as they made their escape had only been her imagination. "Should I ask what she would do to us if she caught us?"

Cerise shook her head without answering, her profile tight in the light of the moons, and the only sound that of their labored breathing.

That's okay, Shreya thought. Probably better she didn't know.

"Do you know where the ships are kept?" Shreya knew whatever sense of direction she'd had about the alien city had been lost as soon as they'd started twisting and turning through the alleyways.

"On the other side, but we can't go through the main streets. Zylia has lots of spies. We need to stick to the alleys and try not to be seen."

Shreya studied the little woman's tense face. "This isn't the first time you've tried to escape, is it?"

After a beat, Cerise shook her head. "I've spent a month in Zylia's dungeon before."

Shreya swallowed hard, her skin going cold, despite the heavy cloak. That was exactly what she hadn't wanted to know, not that she was shocked a creature that traded off the forced sex labor of others would have something so barbaric.

"How long have you been on Lymora III?" she asked, as the alien started walking, and she fell in step next to her.

Cerise bobbled her head. "I don't know. Zylia doesn't allow us to mark time, but at least ten rotations."

Shreya guessed that rotations were the planet's rotation around their sun, or suns. She had no idea how long that was, but from Cerise's expression, it was long enough.

"Don't worry." She squeezed the creature's arm. "This time we won't get caught."

"I can't go back." Cerise's voice had lost its high, chirpy quality. "She'll kill me this time."

Goose pimples formed on Shreya's arms, more from fear than cold, and she rubbed them briskly with her hands. "That's not going to happen. We're both going to get off this planet, and I'm going to take you back to the Boat with me."

"What's the Boat?"

"It's a space station where a lot of aliens live, including a bunch of my friends. There are no pleasure houses and no one is forced to do anything. Plus, they have cool holographic technology so you can recreate almost any setting you can imagine."

Cerise let out a sigh. "No pleasure planets? What do the males do?"

"Either they're mated or they manage to keep it in their pants."

Cerise giggled. "The males from Gondorba would have a hard time with that since they do not wear pants."

"Charming," Shreya said.

"They seem to think so, since they decorate their sex organs with all sorts of ornaments and paint."

Now Shreya laughed. "Of course they do. And they walk around with this dressed-up thing hanging out?"

Cerise's head bobbed up and down. "I wouldn't say it hangs, though. They usually aren't very large."

"That explains the cock costumes."

Cerise giggled again. "You are funny. And nice. I think you are the nicest client we've ever had at the house. That's why I wanted to help you. And because you looked so scared of the big alien with the robot eye."

Shreya's mind went to Vox, and she hoped he was still sleeping peacefully and dreaming of licking whipped cream off her. "He's complicated."

"But you were his prisoner, weren't you? He brought you to Lymora III against your will?"

"Absolutely," Shreya said, "but he wasn't mistreating me, even though he could have."

Cerise picked up her pace, as a pair of tall aliens spilled out of a doorway behind them, laughing and staggering. Shreya matched her, and soon the two women were almost jogging.

"So you did not hate him?" Cerise asked between breaths.

Shreya thought for a moment. She certainly didn't hate Vox. What did she feel about him? Sympathy certainly, since she knew the torment he'd been through. Curiosity, because she wanted to know more about him, and how he'd managed to retain scraps of his former Drexian self, despite all the Kronock brainwashing and experiments. And something else. There was something she felt when he touched her. Something she didn't want to admit to anyone, because it would make her sound crazy. Having feelings for the alien who abducted you was nuts, and getting turned on by the way he touched you was even crazier. No, she was going to keep that to herself.

"I don't hate him, but I'm glad to get away," she finally said, which was the truth. She knew when it came down to it, he was controlled by the Kronock, and they would force him to either turn her over to their labs, or get her knocked up. And she wanted no part of either of those options.

They reached a widening in the passageway, with hulking bins lined against one side, festering trash spilling out of the tops and making Shreya want to gag. She held a hand over her nose as they kept to the far side of the alley. When they'd almost cleared the putrid bins, two massive creatures stepped out from behind the last one and blocked their path.

"Xakden." Cerise's whisper was so soft Shreya barely heard it.

Xakden? That word sounded familiar. She looked away from the enormous beasts for a moment and saw the terrified expression on her companion's face. Hadn't Vox said something about the Xakden when they'd arrived?

She returned her attention to the towering creatures, with horns that curved out of their foreheads and around to the backs of their heads. They were covered with what looked like a layer of brown fuzz, and their arms were thick and hung unusually long by their sides. But what made her mouth go dry was the enormous shape swelling down one side of each of their pant legs.

One of the Xakden took a deep breath through its wet snout. "I can smell their fear, can't you?"

The other grunted in reply, one mitt-sized hand stroking himself through his pants. "And their juices. I want to fuck the big one first. She'll last longer."

The first Xakden jerked his pants down, revealing a cock so massive and thick it made Shreya think of a television program she'd once watched on anacondas. Of course, anacondas didn't have a sharp spike at one end like these monsters apparently did. Vox had not been exaggerating when he said they would split you in two.

Shreya turned to tell Cerise to run, but was pushed roughly to the ground before the words left her lips. She tried to scream for help, but the wind had been knocked out of her, and all she could was gasp for air and hope she died quickly.

Chapter Fourteen

The room was spinning, as Vox woke and found himself on the floor. His shoulder ached, and he assumed he'd rolled off the bed and crashed onto the hard floor. Grasping his throbbing arm, he sat up, blinking to bring the room back into focus.

Where was Shreya? The last thing he remembered he'd been sucking something sweet and creamy off her bare breast. His breath quickened at the memory. She'd covered her own breast in the substance and offered it to him as part of a game. Vox never thought he'd have enjoyed a game as much as he'd liked that one, although he couldn't remember much past that point. His last memory was the feel of her hard nipple between his lips and wanting to taste more of her. Then nothing. Had they…?

Glancing down, he saw he was still wearing pants. He scoured the suite with his gaze. The bed was barely rumpled, and the domed plates remained untouched on the low table. His stomach roiled, as he realized one more thing. Shreya was gone.

Vox pulled himself up, a wave of nausea rising as he stood. Had the cream he'd eaten been bad? His head pounded and his tongue felt thick as he attempted to swallow. Had it been poisoned?

He shook his head. Shreya wouldn't have poisoned him. She wanted him as much as he wanted her. Hadn't her game proven that? Would she have told him to lick food off her if she didn't want him?

Spotting the empty plate on the bed, he frowned. Unless her game had been a ruse meant to distract him. Anger flashed through him. Had she betrayed him? Her absence seemed to prove that, although a small part of him hoped she might have been taken against her will. But who would have done that? No one knew they were there except…

Vox stumbled to the door, and pressed his palm to the surface before yanking it open. He scanned the hall that opened onto the spiraling staircase. Empty. The pink-haired alien who'd been so attentive was nowhere in sight.

"Zylia," he bellowed, his voice echoing through the building and making him press a hand to his temple.

Within moments, the fairy madam appeared from below, her wings fluttering so fast he couldn't see them behind her as she hovered in front of him. Although she smiled, the warmth didn't reach her eyes. "How may I assist Vox of Kronock?"

"My female is gone." He gestured toward his empty suite. "Did you take her?"

The beautiful fairy flipped her lavender hair off one shoulder. "Why would I take your human? I have every room in my house filled with a creature schooled in the arts of pleasure. Your little thing looked like she was too timid to spread her legs."

Vox bristled at the description of his mate. "Then maybe the attendant knows where she went. The one with the pink hair."

Zylia's smile hardened. "Cerise?" She raised her voice and called for the woman again. "Cerise! Come here at once."

No response, although several doors on the hall opened, and brightly painted females in various stages of undress leaned out.

Zylia's smile vanished, and she flew down the circular stairwell so quickly, it took Vox a moment to realize she was gone. He leaned over the gilded railing, peering down to the foyer where he heard Zylia screaming.

"You let them escape, you big oaf!"

Vox took the stairs two at a time as he ran down, ignoring the stares from the occupants of even more open doors at each landing of the spiral staircase. When he reached the dimly lit entry hall, the huge guard was lumbering to his feet and holding his furry head.

"I don't know what happened," he said, his voice gruff.

Zylia flew around him, her arms waving as her wings hummed. "You were tricked, you fool."

The creature looked down. "Sorry, Zylia."

"Did you see anything?" Vox asked.

The guard shook his head without meeting Vox's gaze. "Cerise heard something and asked me to check outside, then she gave me something sweet as a thank you. She always thanks me."

If the alien wasn't covered with black fur, Vox thought he might have been blushing. Clearly, he'd also been fooled by a female he cared about.

"I need to go after my mate," Vox said.

Zylia waved for the guard to open the door. "If you find them, bring me back the other one. I'll make it worth your while."

Vox nodded, noticing the guard flinch. He didn't know if he would bring the little alien back. His priority was finding Shreya, not returning a sex slave to be punished.

Outside the pleasure house, he paused and took in the dark streets lit only by the moons overhead. The main street extended in front of him, but several smaller alleys shot off in different directions. Vox touched a button on the side of his implant. Instantly, a map was projected into his cybernetic eye and directed him to the alley to his left.

When he'd taken the Drexian tracker out of Shreya's neck, he'd added his own. Not a Kronock tracker, but one that sent information to his implant. He'd hoped he wouldn't need it, but he was grateful it now pinpointed where his mate was within the maze of the city.

He ran quickly through the alleys, the buildings rising up several stories on both sides of him and creating the feeling of being in a tunnel. Aside from the occasional puddle or pile of debris, the streets were empty, with most residents and visitors either asleep or passed-out drunk. Few lights shone from windows, and he saw no other creatures in the streets.

That both comforted him and scared him. For one, he was glad there weren't aliens out to harass the two women, but that meant there was also no one to help them if they got into trouble. And on Lymora III, there was always trouble.

Vox cursed himself for bringing Shreya to the lawless, heathen planet. Of all the places for his female to be wandering around, this city would not have been his first choice. Not that a part-Kronock cyborg had many choices when it came to holding females captive in order to mate with them. Not every planet would look kindly on his actions, nor would it welcome him. Here, everyone was wanted for something, so looking the other way was the name of the game.

An alien half his height tripped out of a doorway in front of him, and Vox swerved to avoid flattening him, his heart hammering. He made several sharp turns, wondering why Shreya and the other woman had taken such a circuitous route. He assumed they were heading toward the shipyard, but as he turned once more, he was dismayed to realize that he was running deeper into the roughest part of the city.

Shreya's tracker stopped moving in an alley behind a strip of bars known for being host to the worst of the worst. Vox clenched his fists, pumping them as he ran faster. They would have paused there only if someone or something had stopped them.

The desire to keep her safe was so powerful that nothing else mattered. Not the smell of the trash in the streets, not the sound of his heavy breath, not the pounding of his feet against the stone that rattled his own teeth. He had to protect her. She was his, and he would die before he would let anyone hurt her or take her from him. Even the Kronock.

The thought jolted him, distracting him and making him nearly trip. Bracing a hand against one of the rough walls, he righted himself and kept running. They would come for him. That he knew. And when they saw the human he had taken for Krav's plan, but now wanted for himself, they would take her from him.

A primal roar built deep inside him. Well, the Kronock could not have her. Not for Krav's plan. Not for anything. He wouldn't let them. He wouldn't let them take their offspring, either. If there ever was one. Vox did not care about the plan, or his part in it. Not if it meant losing her.

Thoughts of Shreya flooded his mind and obliterated the sound of General Krav's orders. The smoothness of her skin, the softness of her hair, the feel of the puckered flesh of her breast in his mouth. He would sacrifice everything to get that back.

He turned a corner and almost stumbled over a pile of ruffles sprawled on the ground, with a sweating Xakden bent over it.

"Leave," the Xakden said in a murderous voice. "These are ours."

Vox spotted Shreya on the ground a few feet away, as a slightly smaller Xakden wrestled with both the cloak and the diaphanous layers of her dress while she kicked at him.

Vox tried not to stare at the enormous, fur-covered, spiked phalluses both aliens had freed from their pants—the nearest Xakden dragging his with him as he tried to get astride a flailing Cerise—although he knew they would be easier to defeat since they were fully aroused.

"These are my females," Vox said, seeing Shreya's head snap up when she heard his voice.

"You may have them after we are done," the one struggling with Shreya said, as he dodged her legs and ignored her screams for him to piss off. "There may be something left to stick your cock in."

Blood roared in Vox's head as he attacked, grabbing the first distracted Xakden by the collar and slamming him into the wall, the creature's skull crunching before he slid to the ground in a heap. The other alien glanced up, bellowing when he saw the limp form his friend. He tried to rush at Vox, but his engorged cock was a weight that slowed him down and he only punched the air, the momentum of the failed strike causing him to fall. Vox kicked at the creature until he was coughing green blood, finally taking the furry head in both of his hands and quickly snapping his neck.

He stepped back, breathing heavily, and saw both women gaping at him.

"You saved us," Cerise said, standing up without her fluffy wig, her slightly pointed head tiny and completely smooth.

Shreya was still on the ground, and Vox noticed some blood smeared on the stone beneath her head. He staggered to her, dropping to his knees and cradling her. "Are you hurt?"

She touched a hand to the back of her head. "Nothing serious. Scalp wounds always bleed a lot."

He pulled her close to him, overcome with relief she wasn't seriously injured or ripped in half. After a second, he loosened his grip and looked down at her. "You ran from me."

"It was my idea," Cerise said from behind him. "I convinced her to escape with me. Don't punish her."

Vox swiveled around to see that Cerise had retrieved her wig, and now it sat askew on her head, dirt covering one half of it. "I do not intend to punish her."

"You don't?" Shreya looked at him through narrowed lids. "You're not even going to tie me up again?"

He stood, pulling Shreya with him. "There are no bindings on the ship."

"We're leaving here?" she asked, then glanced at the dead Xakden. "I guess that's probably a good idea, since you just murdered two awfully ugly aliens who probably have a bunch of really mean friends."

"Murder is rarely punished on Lymora III," Vox said, taking her hand snugly in his. "We need to leave so I can keep you out of reach of the Kronock."

Cerise cleared her throat. "I thought *you* were Kronock."

Shreya didn't pull her hand from his. "So did I."

Chapter Fifteen

S hreya's hand shook inside Vox's as she followed blindly behind him. She'd left her cloak on the ground as they'd hurried off, and her teeth chattered even though the planet's suns were starting to rise and burn off the cool of the night. "I don't understand. Now we're running from the Kronock instead of the Drexians?"

She didn't think her head wound was serious, but she was pretty sure she was in mild shock from the attack. The fear of having that huge monster pawing at her and the realization that his raping her would have killed her—and would have been a really painful way to die—had caused a delayed reaction in her body. She gritted her teeth to keep them from rattling.

"The Kronock are more dangerous than the Drexians." He glanced down at her and the pressure on her hand increased. "For you."

They paused where the alleyway spilled into an open square, with a dingy, marble fountain barely spouting water over a pornographic tableau rising up in the center. Although the dawn light cast long shadows, Shreya thought the marble fairy was straddling a shockingly well-endowed centaur, although they were probably statues of alien species' she'd never heard of, and not mythical creatures.

Vox swung his head from side to side, before rushing them across the empty square and down another narrow alley.

"What about that creepy fairy madam?" she asked, glancing over at Cerise, the alien's skirts swinging as she hurried alongside them. "Won't she be looking for her girl?"

"Zylia?" Cerise shuddered. "She would never come out looking, herself. She might send Lar, but he'd never hurt me."

"I'm assuming Lar is the big thing that guards the door?" she asked, rubbing a hand over her goose-pimply arms and remembering the black-haired beast slumped harmlessly against the wall when they'd escaped.

Cerise nodded. "He likes me. More than he likes Zylia."

"I'm sure everyone likes you more than they like Zylia," Shreya said. "Whoever thought fairies were innocent and sweet has never met that one."

"She is not a fairy," Vox said. "She is a Valoushe, and no one ever thought Valoushes were sweet."

Cerise shook her head in obvious agreement with Vox, her dirty pink wig bobbing.

Shreya still couldn't believe that the Kronock hybrid who'd been hell-bent on using her in the plan to destroy the Drexians and Earth was now helping her escape. She'd been convinced he would have been livid at her for tricking him, drugging him, and running away from the pleasure house. As grateful as she was he'd killed those terrifying Xakden, she'd fully expected him to drag her back and chain her to the bed for good.

Her hand that was tucked into his was the only part of her body that wasn't freezing, and the heat felt comforting as she struggled to keep her trembling under control. She cut her eyes to Vox's bare chest, a sheen of sweat on his bronze, sculpted muscles. How was he not turning blue?

"Shreya." His voice caused her to wrench her eyes from him, and she realized that they'd stopped in the middle of a passageway.

She met his gaze. "I'm sorry. What?"

"You're shaking, and you haven't responded to my questions." He moved his hands to her arms, his brows pressing together. "You are too cold."

She nodded, a wave of dizziness making her sway. "I might be going into shock." She tried to smile. "It's been a stressful few days."

Scooping her up in his arms, he pressed her to his chest, then looked down at Cerise. "Please tell me you are not also going into shock. I do not know how I can carry you both."

Cerise giggled. "No, I'm fine."

Shreya pulled her arms into her chest, her face pressed against the heat of his body. He might be part Kronock and part cyborg, but his skin was incredibly soft. "Thank you."

He glanced down at her, his red cybernetic eye pulsing. "For what?"

She closed her eyes and inhaled the scent of his skin, which was musky and male and not at all artificial. "For changing your mind."

He did not respond, but she felt him start walking again. The warmth of his arms around her and the soothing rhythm of his long strides soon had her breathing and her body temperature returning to normal.

Shreya took deep breaths and, after a while, she noticed that the scent of stale alcohol and festering garbage had been replaced by the faint smell of burning fuel. Opening her eyes, she saw that they were on the edge of the city where the streets opened out onto the shipyard. Even at the early hour, there was movement, as aliens disembarked and headed into the city.

She tapped Vox's chest. "I should probably walk on my own."

He did not relax his grip. "Why? You entered the city thrown over my shoulder. No one will think it odd to see me carrying a female to my ship."

"Maybe not, but I'd still like to walk. I feel a lot better now." She was also not used to being treated like an invalid or a helpless female. If she could walk, she wanted to walk.

Vox gently set her on the ground, standing awkwardly in front of her for a moment before she took his hand. The air wasn't as turbulent as it had been when they'd arrived, but dust still kicked up from the ground, and most of the aliens hurrying around them wore coverings over their faces.

"So which one is yours?" Cerise asked, her hand over her nose as she surveyed the spaceships being refueled and repaired on the wide, dusty stretch of land.

Vox pointed to the gray ship that appeared to be covered in scales. In contrast to some of the sleek, curved ships around it, the Kronock ship was all sharp angles and jutting points.

Since she'd been unconscious when she'd boarded the ship and bouncing over his shoulder when she'd left, Shreya hadn't gotten a good look at it before now. She didn't know how a ship could look menacing, but this one did.

Vox began walking toward it, tugging her along with him. "We shouldn't delay."

"If this is a Kronock ship, won't the Kronock be able to track it?"

she asked, her stomach tightening at the thought that if turnabout was fair play, Vox might be tricking her.

They reached the ship, and Shreya thought it was even bigger and scarier up close, her mouth going dry at the thought of willingly going inside.

Vox dropped her hand and opened a panel underneath the ship, bending down low and peering up into the innards of the vessel. He pulled out a small, black box, no larger than a matchbook, with a blinking, blue light in one corner. "The tracker."

Instead of crushing it under his heel, he glanced furtively around them before walking over to the ship next to them and tucking it inside the open ramp. He returned and activated his own ship's ramp, which lowered to the ground. "Now they will not be able to find us."

"You're sending them on a wild-goose chase," she said. "Not bad."

He cocked is head at her. "I do not know this 'wild goose.' Is it very ferocious?"

She grinned. "Ferocious? Not exactly. It's an Earth expression that means you're making them waste their time going after something they can't catch."

"I like your Earth expressions," Cerise said, her high heels echoing off the metal ramp as she started to walk up. "Maybe we could go there."

Shreya could imagine the panic that would ensue if they flew down to Earth in a scaly, alien spaceship, and she disembarked with a tiny alien with shimmering, blue skin, and another who was part cyborg. It would not go well for anyone.

She followed Cerise up the ramp. "I don't think that's a great idea. Earth doesn't know aliens exist."

Cerise turned and gaped at her. "Earthlings believe they are alone in the universe?"

"Most of them," Shreya admitted, prodding Cerise to keep walking. "I know it sounds weird, but if you believe in aliens on Earth, you're considered crazy."

"Then how did you get here?" Cerise asked, once they'd reached the inside of the ship.

Shreya looked at Vox as his heavy boots thudded up the ramp. "It's a really long story."

"I suggest you both strap in, or find something to hold onto," he said, his expression serious. "It might not be a smooth departure."

Shreya watched him disappear into the front of the ship, then turned back to Cerise. "What do you think that was all about?"

The alien pointed outside. Though her view was shrinking as the ramp lifted, Shreya saw several figures running toward them, waving their arms and pointing blasters. One of them was huge and covered in black fur, his face clearly twisted in agony as he watched the metal ramp clamp shut with Cerise inside.

Chapter Sixteen

Vox dropped into the pilot's seat, pulling the straps over his chest as he tapped his fingers on the console to power up the ship. He'd seen Zylia's guard heading their way, along with what looked like some of the Lymora III enforcers. He knew the armed security force on the renegade planet was used primarily for keeping visitor's ships from being stolen, but he suspected Zylia had bribed them to keep him grounded. Even though he'd paid for his suite in advance, he suspected Cerise was more valuable to the Valoushe than she'd let on. That, or she relished the woman's punishment. Knowing Zylia, it was probably the latter.

Shreya skidded to a stop as she ran into the cockpit, the gauzy white fabric of her dress swirling around her legs. "You know we're being fired on, right?"

"Blasters only," he said, as the engines spun up and hummed beneath his feet.

"I take it the shielding on this thing can withstand blaster fire?"

He gave a snort of laughter. "The hull will be undamaged by their blasters." He jerked a head to the chair next to him. "Take a seat."

She sat down, fumbling with the straps until he stilled her hands and quickly fastened her to the chair. He did not want her flying across the cockpit, and he knew their take-off would be rough.

"Cerise is still here?" he asked, flipping a switch and feeling himself pressed into the seat as the ship shot off the ground.

"I'm here," her voice was high and breathy.

Vox turned to see her clutching one of the bench seats that ran perpendicularly behind them, and he snatched a handful of her skirt's fabric before she slid off the end and hit the floor. "Strap in."

She nodded, her bright-pink bow of a mouth open in a perfect O as the ship soared through the atmosphere, and they emerged into the blackness of space in a matter of seconds. He released her and turned back to the console, setting in a course and hoping Zylia hadn't made it worth the enforcers' while to pursue them off the planet.

Bracing himself for incoming fire, he accelerated the ship until he was sure they were far enough away that the Lymorans hadn't pursued or they'd outrun the inferior vessels.

"So where are we going?" Shreya asked after a few minutes.

He wasn't sure. He'd set a course away from the planet, but not to a specific destination. "I don't know."

"But not the Kronock?" she asked, her voice hesitant.

He looked at her, seeing her nibbling the corner of her mouth. "No, not the Kronock. I told you, I will keep you safe from them."

She nodded, but did not look convinced. Vox knew that after everything that had happened between them, she did not fully trust him. He understood. He was barely able to trust his own feelings, knowing how strong the pull of the Kronock had been, and how deeply his mission had been engrained in him. But as he looked at her and felt heat stirring in his core, he knew his desire for Shreya was stronger than any indoctrination.

A flash of pain made him jerk back against the seat, gripping the armrests tightly until it passed. Even if he could overcome the thoughts that had been drilled into him, he could not escape the device they'd implanted in his head.

Releasing his restraints, he stood and headed for the back of the ship, ignoring both females staring at him in silence. Maybe there was something in a med kit that could help him.

When Vox reached the center of the ship, a round space with short spokes leading off it, he tilted his head back to the steel mesh that held supplies strapped to the ceiling. Even though he was over six and a half feet tall, the Kronock were taller, so he needed to stretch his arms high to pull down the black box.

Another pain seared through his brain, causing him to stumble and drop the kit.

"Why don't I help you?" Shreya said, picking up the kit and holding his arm to steady him.

"I was looking for pain inhibitors," he said, watching her snap open the box.

She nodded as she bent down, opening the box and pawing through the contents. "I don't suppose these pain inhibitors look like Advil."

"Ad-vil?"

She waved a hand over her head without looking up. "Never mind. Another Earth thing. So what do they look like?"

Vox rubbed his temple. "Black needles with a red tip."

"Seriously?" Shreya held up one long, dark syringe. "You guys are hard core."

"It needs to be injected in my neck. Can you do it?"

"My test subjects are usually significantly smaller, but I should be able to do this."

He didn't understand her words, but steeled himself for the pinch as she counted out loud and then jabbed him in the neck. The chemical was cool as it entered his system, and his muscles immediately relaxed.

She packed up the med kit and clamped it shut, eyeing him as she handed it back. "Are you sure you're okay?"

"You are worried about my well-being?"

She cleared her throat. "That, and I don't exactly want to be flying through space without a pilot. Cerise is great, but I think she knows about as much about spaceships as I do, which is not much."

He tucked the med kit back under the steel netting overhead. "I promise I will not leave you to captain the ship."

She peered up at him from under dark lashes. "And thanks for not holding me to the other promise."

Vox tilted his head at her. "What other promise?"

"You know." She looked down at her feet. "The one about me letting you…"

He stepped closer to her. "The promise that I will not force you, if you will let me touch and taste you as much as I want?"

She backed up until she was against one of the textured, gunmetal-gray walls. "I thought since you weren't keeping me in that house and you weren't going to turn me over to the Kronock…"

Vox brushed her hair away from her face. "You are right that I have no intention of letting the Kronock use you for their plan, but that is because I want you for myself. When I claim you, it will not be for the Kronock empire, it will be for me. I want every moan and every gasp as I take you to be for me alone."

Her mouth fell open, and his gaze went to her soft, pink lips.

"When I thought you might be hurt, I felt something I'd never felt before." He took her jaw in his hand, dragging his thumb across her bottom lip. "I knew that you were meant to be mine, and it is my destiny to protect you. I also knew that you were meant to be my mate for life, and I would never let anyone else touch you."

Her breath was shallow as he lifted her face to his. "That doesn't sound like a Kronock talking."

"You seem to have brought out the Drexian in me."

Her dark eyes flashed, and he saw the hunger in them. She wanted him as much as he wanted her, although he could tell she was fighting her urges.

"I wasn't even a tribute bride," she said. "I'm not supposed to be a Drexian's mate."

"Do you think I care about any of that?" He was so close to her, he could feel her soft, warm breath against his own lips. "All I know is that you will always be mine."

Before he could give her another reason, Shreya crushed her mouth to his. It took him a moment to realize she was kissing him wildly, her tongue parting his mouth, and her hands raking his hair.

Vox reached down with both hands and lifted her so that her legs were wrapped around his waist, pressing her against the wall, his cock throbbing. Long-buried emotions swirled in his head, as he drank in the taste of her.

This human with the long, dark hair and soft, brown skin was his to claim. His hunger for her felt raw and primal as he ground his body against hers and heard her moan. Whatever part of him was cybernetic, it was not the part that was flooded with blinding desire. He was aware of nothing but the feel of her lush body, the taste of her sweet tongue tangling with his, and the sound of her desperate breaths.

He pulled back, her pants filling his ears. "Tell me."

She tipped her head back, her eyes dazed. "Tell you what?"

"Tell me you want me to claim you." He saw her pupils dilate, and he lowered his head until his lips touched the petal-softness of her ear. "Tell me you want me inside you."

Her body jerked, but he did not release his grip on her. "I can feel how much you want me. Why are you fighting it, Shreya?"

"I shouldn't want you." Her words were barely a whisper.

"But you do. You know that you're mine, and I was meant to be inside you, claiming you as my mate." His tongue flicked the edge of her ear. "Fucking you hard."

Her entire body convulsed, and her fingers bit into his back. "Yes, Vox."

"Yes, what?" he prodded, arching his back as her fingers scraped over his fiery nodes.

She took his face in her hands, her gaze molten as their eyes met. "I want you. *Now*."

Chapter Seventeen

Shreya could hear nothing but the roar of blood in her ears as he pulled her dress off her, his large hands ripping at the straps and tugging the layered fabric until she stood naked in the middle of the ship's entryway.

The thought of Cerise floated briefly through her brain. Where was she? As a veteran of an alien whorehouse, Shreya suspected she'd grown accustomed to staying out of the way when things got hot and heavy, although she doubted many clients got it on in the foyer of the house.

Her cheeks flamed as she realized she was in the middle of the ship with nothing on, but the moment of embarrassment passed when she remembered only three beings were on board, and one of them was the gorgeous, ripped alien who'd practically torn her clothes off her.

Vox's gaze raked over her body, and she barely noticed the red flash of his cybernetic eye. All she could see was the vein pulsing in his thick neck, and the fierce set of his jaw as he looked at her like a predator about to strike. He ran both hands down the sides of her body until he reached the swell of her hips, and he jerked her toward him. "You are mine. No one else's."

Normally, the straight-A, overachieving, women-can-do-anything-men-can-do version of herself would have bristled at the caveman sentiment, but she reveled in her surrender to him. She knew she shouldn't savor the feeling of this huge, part-cyborg alien declaring that she belonged to him, but she did. She loved the way he looked at her and the way he wanted her—desperately and without any hesitation.

Something in him had changed since he'd first stolen her off the Drexian ship. She could see it in his eyes and hear it in his voice. Maybe it was a result of the Kronock DNA degrading and the Drexian DNA asserting itself, or maybe it was his real personality bubbling up from under the layers of brainwashing, but whatever the reason, she knew he was different. She knew he wouldn't hurt her, or let anyone else hurt her.

This was what she'd never had, a man so mad for her that he'd sacrifice everything to be with her. She'd never experienced anything close to this type of passion and obsession and desire, and she wanted it more than she'd ever wanted anything.

Her body melted into his. "Only yours, Vox."

His mouth crashed onto hers. If he hadn't been holding her, Shreya's knees would have given way. Though his mouth was insistent, his lips were soft and his tongue gentle as it stroked hers, sending ripples of pleasure down her spine.

Through her daze, she felt his hands move down to cup her ass. He lifted her, and she let her legs fall open before wrapping them around him.

Vox moved her so that her opening pressed again something thick and hard. Bloody hell, was that his cock? He rocked her against the length of him as he let out a low moan. Panic fluttered in her stomach, and she pulled back.

"You're really big," she said, catching her breath.

His own breath was ragged. "You do not like big?"

"It's just…" Her cheeks burned. "I don't know if I can take all of you."

"We will start small," he said, sliding his hand so that his fingers teased her wet opening.

She gasped as he slipped one thick finger inside her. "Nothing about you is very small."

"You are small." He buried his face in her neck with a groan. "And so warm and wet for me."

She couldn't help moving up and down on his finger, loving the sensation of stretching around him as he slid a second finger inside her. Moaning, she swiveled her hips, her hands gripping the slick, taut muscles of his shoulders for leverage.

As she moved faster, she reached around and found his nodes. Her fingers brushed one hot, hard bump, and Vox nipped her neck in response.

"You like that?" she whispered, circling a node with her fingertip and feeling it pulse.

A growl built deep in his chest, and he matched her pace as he pumped his fingers inside her. She rocked into him, her breaths jagged gasps as need and desire overtook her.

The curved metal of the ship echoed their moans and panting back to them, and the magnified sounds of their pleasure aroused her even more. She was already teetering on the edge, when he slipped one finger out of her, sliding it up to stroke her clit. The pad of his finger circled her slick bundle of nerves quickly, while also pivoting the finger still lodged inside her.

Her body detonated, her legs clamping him in a vise and her nails scoring his back as her muscles tensed around his finger again and again. Vox held her, his finger still caressing her clit while the other moved inside her until she sagged in his arms.

Her heart raced, as she reached down and started unbuttoning his pants.

"You are ready?" he asked, his own breath uneven.

She nodded. What she'd gotten was just a taste, and she needed more. She needed to feel his cock inside her, even if it was huge. When she unfastened his pants, he lifted her so that they dropped to his ankles.

Shreya was startled to see that he wasn't wearing underwear, and wondered if it was a Drexian thing—although she felt sure she'd have heard a whisper about that on the Boat if going commando was a species trait—or a Kronock thing, or just a Vox thing.

Once she'd gotten past the no-underwear situation, she got her first full glimpse of his cock. She couldn't even try to play it cool, as her mouth fell open. Standing out ramrod straight, it was long and thick, with veins running down the dark-bronze length. She felt a moment of relief that there was nothing cybernetic about it, although that didn't make it less intimidating.

"I will go slow," he murmured into her ear, then kissed his way across her jawline before capturing her mouth in his again.

His deep, sensual kisses distracted her, and she was only vaguely aware of being pressed harder against the wall. Her heart hammered in her chest as Vox dragged the tip of his cock through her slick folds. Panic mingled with desire, and she tried to pull away, but he kissed her more deeply, his tongue swirling with hers as he slowly pushed into her.

Even with only the crown of his cock inside, Shreya felt herself stretching painfully. Thoughts flooded her mind as she tried to move away from him. She couldn't do this. He was too big. She didn't know what she'd been thinking to try to take an alien as big as him.

She finally wrenched herself away. "Vox, I can't."

He met her gaze, drawing one finger over her bottom lip. "Shreya, you are mine." With his other hand, he held her body steady as he thrust into her.

Air rushed out of her lungs as his cock filled her. She could feel herself stretching to take all of him, and her legs instinctively clamped around his waist. He held himself inside her as she grasped his shoulders, her arms shaking. After a moment, the discomfort went away, and then there was only the amazing feeling of being completely filled by him.

"Are you okay?" he asked.

She let out a deep sigh. "Better than okay." She shifted, feeling his girth thick and hard inside her. "You feel so good."

The veins in his neck pulsed, as he clenched his teeth.

"Are you okay?" she asked, watching a bead of sweat trickle down the hollow of his throat.

"You're so tight." The words escaped him in gasps.

Even though he didn't move, Shreya lifted herself and sank down again. Vox dropped his head back and let out a guttural sound, spurring her to do it again. She'd thought being filled by him felt good, but this felt even better.

He grasped her hips and lifted her even higher, bringing her down hard on his cock. "You like this?"

She couldn't speak, she could only moan in response as they moved together to pump her up and down, moving faster and harder until the sound of skin slapping skin was almost as loud as her cries of pleasure.

"I want to see." His voice was raw as he stepped back and tilted her body out so he could look down and see where his cock impaled her.

Instead of being embarrassed, Shreya loved the idea of him watching and she dropped her own eyes. "See how tight I'm stretched around your huge cock?"

He made a strangled noise, dragging himself almost all the way out and then slowly plunging back in. "You are mine." He pumped again. "All of you is mine."

"Yes, Vox." She couldn't imagine anything ever feeling as good as this, as a scorching heat tore through her and she reared up, bucking as she clawed at his shoulders.

He pistoned into her a few more times until he let out a roar that rattled the walls, and a warm heat pulsed inside her. After a final tremble, he braced one palm against the wall and leaned her against it.

Shreya sagged forward, resting her cheek on his chest and hearing the knocking of his heart. Her entire body shook, and she was pretty sure she wouldn't be able to walk for days. She also knew one thing for sure. There was no going back now.

Chapter Eighteen

Vox held Shreya to his chest with one arm, even though he was afraid his legs might buckle if he did not release her. He didn't want the feeling to end, and he loved feeling her heart beat and hearing her panting for breath. It was enough to make him want to start moving her on his cock again, since he was still inside her and still hard.

"You can let me down if you need to," she said, her breath coming out in soft puffs against his chest.

"I am fine," he said.

She laughed. "I can feel your legs shaking, Vox."

Only when she mentioned it did he notice the trembling in his legs, his muscular thighs twitching as if he'd run a long race. "If I do, can you stand?"

She lifted her head from his chest, and he immediately missed the warmth of her cheek. "Stand, yes. Walk? I'm not so sure." She gasped as he shifted his grip on her hips. "Do Drexians not go soft, or is it a Kroock thing? Or a cyborg thing?"

"Soft?" He saw her eyes dart down and realized what she meant.

"Oh. I guess it is a Drexian thing. We can go several times before losing hardness."

She murmured something under her breath he thought might be a human curse, but she did not sound angry.

"Does it bother you?" he asked, hoping he was not hurting her.

"Bother me?" Her already flushed cheeks became pinker. "Not exactly, but I don't know if I'll survive several more times. At least not right now."

"We do not have to." His gaze wandered to the hard points of nipples, the skin dusky but flushed. He wanted to take them in his mouth, but he knew then he would not be able to stop himself from pinning her to the wall again. Even the thought of tasting her made his cock twitch and made Shreya suck in breath.

Although he hated the idea of not being inside her, he gingerly lifted her off his stiff cock and lowered her feet to the floor. She leaned into him as she regained her balance, and he wrapped both arms around her. Being inside her had been the best thing he'd ever felt, but he also liked holding her like that, her small body pressed against his.

After a few deep breaths, she cleared her throat. "I can't believe we did that."

"Did you not like it?"

"Oh, I liked it. I didn't know I could like it *that* much."

He tightened his arms around her. "Then you would like to do it again?"

She laughed again. "Do you want to do it again?"

He put his hand under her chin and lifted her face so she was looking up at him. "You are mine, Shreya. I plan to take you so many times you will forget there was ever anyone but me."

She blinked quickly, her eyes shining, then she pulled him down and into a deep kiss that he felt in the tips of his toes.

"I hate to interrupt." Cerise's high voice broke the spell, and Shreya jumped back.

Vox could see the back of the alien's pink wig as she faced away from them in the passageway leading to the cockpit. Shreya darted around the circular space, snatching her dress off the floor and pulling it on quickly.

"Sorry we left you, Cerise," she said. "We were—"

Cereise waved a tiny hand over her head. "You don't have to explain to me. I spent the past three years in a pleasure house, remember?"

"Right." Shreya motioned for him to pull up his pants, her gaze lingering for a moment on his cock, still slick with her juices, and her cheeks coloring.

"I wouldn't bother you two, but I think we might have a tail."

Vox pushed his cock down to get it inside his pants before he fastened them. "A tail?"

"Another ship following us."

He took long steps, striding past Cerise and heading for the cockpit. When he lowered himself into the pilot's chair and scanned the readouts, he saw what she was talking about. It was far away, but there was a ship's signature on an intercept course.

He tapped a few buttons on the console. It was too far away for him to determine if the course was a coincidence, or if the ship was actually trying to intercept them. He also couldn't get a clear signature reading from the vessel. It could be a ship from Lymora III, although he doubted it, or it could be the Kronock coming after him to ensure he followed their orders. That was more likely…and more worrying.

He glanced back at Shreya as she entered the cockpit and joined him at the console. Her hair fell wild around her shoulders and her shoulder straps were tied unevenly, making it all but obvious she'd just been fucked. She lowered herself gently into the chair, and he knew it was because she was sore from his cock.

Vox felt a rush of protectiveness. Before, he'd felt she was his. Now that he had claimed her, he knew it with every fiber of his being. Shreya was his mate to protect, even with his life.

"It is probably nothing." He gave what he hoped was a reassuring nod, as he changed their course to see if the other ship would follow.

After a minute, the other ship altered course to match theirs, and increased its speed.

"*Grek.*" He knew he could not outrun a Kronock ship, especially if it was a newer one. The ship they were in—the one he'd commandeered when he'd taken Shreya away from the Kronock research outpost—was little more than a glorified transport ship. It wasn't designed for speed, or battles, or even for stealth.

"What?" Shreya asked.

"It might be the Kronock," he admitted. He didn't want to lie to her. "They might have found us, even without the ship's tracker."

Shreya glanced over at him, her eyes resting on his cybernetic implant. "There's one tracker you can't get rid of."

His fingers went to the metal implant over his eye, and a pain shot through his head. He pinched the bridge of his nose and squeezed his eyes shut, fighting the urge to scream.

She was right. He'd been a fool to think the Kronock weren't tracking him and monitoring his every move. They'd put too much into him to let him go, and General Krav would have installed fail-safes and backup ways to monitor him. Why hadn't he realized it before? He was never going to get away from the aliens who'd tortured him, destroying who he'd been and leaving a part-cyborg monster in his place. He would never get to be with his mate. Not unless it was observing her in a lab while she grew hybrid babies for the Kronock.

"Vox?" Her hand touched his shoulder. "Are you okay?"

He jerked away. This was all his fault. He'd taken her, and now they were going to take her from him. His mind flashed back to the feeling of being inside her and the feeling of holding her. He leapt up, ignoring the look of shock and hurt on Shreya's face.

He wasn't going to let them have her. Shreya was his. She would always be his, even if he was gone.

Stomping out of the cockpit and passing an open-mouthed Cerise, he headed for the back of the ship. There was only one option. He had to leave the ship so they couldn't track it any longer. With him gone, the two women had a chance of escaping.

He walked down one of the spokes that extended off the main compartment of the ship until he reached the escape pods. There were two of the bullet-shaped pods, but he only needed one.

He took a shuddering breath. The pods were designed to be jettisoned toward a planet, but there was no nearby planet for him to land on. No, he'd just be floating in space until the Kronock found him. He pushed aside the fear of drifting alone with limited oxygen. It was only way Shreya would have a chance of being free, even if it meant never seeing her again.

He doubted he'd live long once the Kronock ascertained his treason. Or if they did let him live, he knew he would pay for his duplicity in almost unbearable torture. Clenching his teeth, he leaned one hand on the cool, gray scale-like hull of the escape pod and snapped open the lid. If he could save Shreya, it would be worth it.

Chapter Nineteen

Shreya exchanged a glance with Cerise once Vox had stormed out of the cockpit. "You have more experience with alien races than I do. Are they all so dramatic?"

Cerise giggled, her iridescent skin glowing faintly blue in the lights of the console. "This one likes to be loud." She gave Shreya a side-eye glance. "Although I wouldn't say you're quiet."

A flush crawled up Shreya's neck to her face. "I don't know what got into me."

"I think it was fairly obvious what was in—"

Shreya cut her off. "I mean, I can't believe I actually did that. In the middle of the ship. Up against a wall. With the cyborg hybrid who abducted me."

Cerise twitched one of her shoulders up. "Why not? As you said, I've seen a lot of aliens, and he's one of the best-looking ones I've ever laid eyes on. Why wouldn't you want to have a ride?"

Shreya gave a shake of her head. "I've never thought about it like that."

"Like what?" Cerise cocked her head, and her wig slipped an inch or two down the side of her head.

"I don't know." Shreya turned her attention to the narrow view out the front of the ship, as stars became streaks of light shooting by. "As something that wasn't a big deal."

"It doesn't have to be a big deal, although I can tell you it's a big deal to him."

Shreya swung her head back around to look at the woman. "Why do you say that?"

Cerise laughed. "Don't you see the way he looks at you? No male looks at a female that way if he's just in it for the fun. Trust me. I see aliens who want only fun every day. This one wants more. And if I'm right, a lot more."

"He keeps saying I'm his mate for life."

Cerise let out a low whistle. "That would be more."

"But I can't be his mate for life. As amazing as the sex was—and it was amazing—he's still a Kronock hybrid who wants me to create the next generation of human-Kronocks so they can destroy the Drexians and my home planet."

Cerise drummed her stubby fingers on the stiff ruffles of her skirt. "That does put a damper on things." Her gaze went to Shreya's stomach. "So if he just impregnated you, the Kronock are going to take the baby?"

Shreya's hands flew to her midriff. "I can't be… He wouldn't let them do that."

Cerise didn't respond. Shreya had been too caught up in the moment to give a second thought to the possibility that she could get pregnant. Of course she knew it was possible. She wasn't clueless. Just stupid, she thought. And incredibly horny.

Her stomach tightened into a ball. Even if she had gotten pregnant from the first time with Vox, he'd never let the Kronock take her or the baby. Would he? Would he have a choice? If it really was a Kronock ship after them, would they stand a chance fighting them off?

Shreya knew he was becoming more and more Drexian as the Kronock DNA was denigrating, but he'd still been brainwashed. He'd never said exactly what they'd done to him, but she suspected it had been intense. Would he be able to fight it enough to protect her, or had she fallen victim to his long game?

She balled one hand into a fist. No. She refused to believe Vox was conning her. Hadn't Cerise said it was clear how he felt about her? And she felt it, too. She knew she'd become more than a captive to him. She swallowed hard. And bloody hell if he hadn't become more than her cyborg captor. Much more.

"Idiot," she whispered to herself. How had she allowed herself to fall for him? This complicated everything.

Glancing down at the star chart displayed on the console, she could see the blinking dot of the other ship closing the distance between them. She stood quickly, and Cerise glanced up at her.

"I need to find Vox," she said, stomping out of the cockpit almost as forcefully as he had.

She didn't believe he was working for the Kronock anymore, and she felt fairly confident he wouldn't let them take her, but none of that mattered if he was a living, breathing beacon who would lead the enemy to her every time. And even if they ran from this Kronock ship, there would be others. She'd learned enough about the violent aliens to know they'd never give up.

It didn't matter how many Drexian memories or feelings returned to Vox. As long as he had that implant, he was controllable by the

Kronock, and she was in danger. Her fingers reflexively touched her stomach. And she might not be the only one.

She stormed down the corridor and into the circular center of the ship, her gaze resting briefly on the wall she'd recently been pressed against. There was a rush of heat between her legs that made her lose a step. *Focus, Shreya.*

She paused and scanned the spokes extending from the center. When she finally heard movement coming from one, she hurried down. What was Vox doing down there while the enemy was closing in on them?

When she spotted him standing in front of an open pod, it took her a moment to figure out what it was and what was going on. When she put it all together, she wanted to punch him.

"You're abandoning us?"

He flinched but didn't turn. "I'm giving you and Cerise a chance. You and I both know they can keep tracking me no matter how many devices I rip out of ships. If I leave, they'll track me and you two can get away."

"So that's it? You were going to launch yourself out an escape pod without even telling me? After what we just…" Her voice cracked. "After everything?"

He turned slowly, and she saw that his face was contorted in pain. "It's the only way I know to keep you safe. I have to protect you, even from myself."

Her gaze went to the small pod. "How would you even navigate in there?"

"It's not designed for navigation. It's designed for retrieval."

She swallowed the lump in her throat. "So the Kronock would retrieve you and then what? They shoot you full of their DNA again, and you go back to being one of their automatons? You go back to your master plan? If I get away, will they have to kidnap another human for you to impregnate?"

He shook his head, but she thought it was more to convince himself than to convince her. "There is no one for me but you."

"I doubt your scaly friends feel the same way."

"But you will be safe." Now his voice cracked as he closed the distance between them and touched a hand to her face. "That is what matters, keeping you from them."

"You matter, too."

His hand twitched against her cheek. "I am lost. There is nothing I can do about what they've done to me, but I can keep them from doing anything to you."

She shook her head hard. "I don't accept that. You aren't lost. I've seen who you really are beneath the implant and the brainwashing and the torture. There's still a Drexian under there."

He cupped her face and stroked his thumb across her jaw. "It doesn't matter. They made me one of them. They will always come for me, and anyone who is near me will be hurt. I would rather die than let them hurt you, Shreya." He leaned down and kissed her softly. "You need to let me go."

Her knees almost buckled as her entire body buzzed from his touch. "No way," she whispered when he pulled away. "I don't know exactly what this is." She waved a hand between them. "But I know I've never felt anything close to it before, and I'm not giving up on it. I'm not giving up on you."

His brow creased into deep furrows. "If I stay here, they'll capture us all."

She took a deep breath. "I'm not going to let that happen. I'm a scientist. I was on that ship you took me from because I'd been studying you and what the Kronock did to you. I think I can help."

He stepped away from her and dropped his hand from her face, his expression stunned.

Chapter Twenty

"**Y**ou are a scientist?" Vox stared at her. She was a scientist and she'd been studying *him?*

Shreya nodded.

He shook his head, as if trying to loosen something. "I did not know human females were scientists."

"Not all of us are. Actually, not all that many are, especially not on the Boat. I know I'm the only microbiologist."

He worked the word over in his mind—microbiologist. His mate was a microbiologist? "And you have been studying me? How?"

She let out a breath. "The Drexians got their hands on a bunch of Kronock records detailing what they did to you to make you…" she hesitated "…more like them."

"And?"

"And I discovered your body is rejecting the Kronock DNA, which is causing your original DNA to degenerate. I was on the rescue ship so I could help stabilize you."

He scowled. "So I am becoming less Kronock?"

"I think," she said. "Even though at first, the Kronock DNA was dominant and your body started changing, after a certain point it started to be less and less effective. I suspect they've been giving you injections to keep you stable."

Vox flinched. "Yes. Many injections and procedures." He rubbed his arms, his hands bumping over the scaly patches. "So if I do not get more injections. . .?"

"I don't know for sure, but I think your body will degrade to a point that your organs may start shutting down."

He nodded and cleared his throat. "So I must return to the Kronock for more procedures and more Kronock DNA, or I will die."

"Or we could go to the Drexian space station." She reached a hand out to touch his arm. "I have a lab, and I could stabilize you using Drexian DNA, instead."

He cringed, pulling his arm away from her. "To them, I am a criminal. A traitor."

Shreya shook her head insistently. "No, you're not. They know you were captured and tortured. The Drexians don't blame you for being brainwashed."

"They will blame me for taking you." His gaze met hers. "Or trying to force you. For attempting to make you part of the Kronock plan to destroy them."

She stepped closer. "But you didn't force me. Your Drexian side wouldn't let you. And you were about to jettison yourself into space to keep me safe from the Kronock."

Vox shook his head slowly. "I have done too much. I have betrayed my own kind and worked for the enemy. For a Drexian, there is nothing worse than that."

"It wasn't your fault you were brainwashed." Her voice got louder.

"You didn't ask to be taken captive or to have that thing put in your head. I promise they won't punish you for those things. I won't let them."

He cocked any eyebrow. "They will listen to you? Are you very important on the Boat?"

Her eyes flickered. "Important enough to make them understand." She took his hand and squeezed it. "You have to trust me, Vox."

He looked into her brown eyes. He wanted to believe her, to trust her, but she'd been hiding such a big secret from him. She'd known all along why he was getting blinding pains, and she hadn't told him. She hadn't helped him. The realization was a punch to the gut.

If she'd been keeping such a big part of herself from him, how much more was she hiding? Was anything she'd told him true, or had she done everything only to get away from him? She'd staged an elaborate game just so she could drug him and escape with Cerise. Sure, she'd come with him to the ship, but had she really had a choice after she'd almost been torn apart by the Xakden? And now she was claiming she could help him by taking him to the Drexians? How could he be sure this wasn't another trick?

But did he really blame her for not trusting him and trying to escape? He *had* abducted her and tied her up to a bed with the purpose of forcing her to mate with him. Would he have wanted to help someone who did that to him? Probably not, he admitted to himself.

"Even if I agree to go back to the Boat with you, we still can't escape from the Kronock," he said, tapping his implant. "They're tracking me."

She glanced up at his cybernetic eye. "I think I might be able to disable that."

One hand rose to touch the cool metal. "How?"

"By removing it," she said.

"Microbiologists work with cybernetics?"

"Well, no." She dropped her eyes. "I have observed a lot of surgeries. I didn't know if I wanted to be a doctor or go into microbiology for a while, so I shadowed a friend who was a resident in a hospital."

He stared at her. "You have only observed surgeries?"

"Yes, but I'm a really quick learner."

"Did any of these surgeries involve implants?" Vox asked.

"Not exactly," she said. "At least not the kind you have. Earth hasn't developed that type of technology yet, at least not that they use on people."

He gaped at her. "This is how you convince me?"

"I'm trying to be honest," Shreya said. "I'm not saying it's the best option, but it seems better to me than you being taken by the Kronock again, or all of us being captured by them."

He supposed she was right about that, but he still was not sure if she was being completely honest with him. More than anything, Vox wanted to believe she was doing all this to help him, but how much did he really know about her? Not much, it turned out. She wasn't just a pretty human. She was a scientist who'd been studying him. She'd been on a mission to capture him, and now she was trying to convince him to surrender to the Drexians.

When he'd been inside her, he'd felt like they were one. Nothing had felt more right to him than when she'd surrendered to him completely. Now he wondered if her cries of pleasure had been real.

"Vox." Her voice startled him.

He focused on her, and her intense gaze.

"I can't lose you," she said. "Please let me try to save you."

His throat constricted. She was right. This was the only chance he had to avoid being taken back to the Kronock, and it would keep her safe. Even if it was a trick to get him back to the Drexians to stand trial for treason, he didn't care. Despite everything, he had to keep her safe. That hadn't changed for him.

He looked deep into her dark eyes. How he felt for her hadn't changed, either. He couldn't unwind his heart from hers now even if he wanted to, which he didn't. She was his—always. Which meant he was also hers. He knew he'd never regret their moments of passion or how she was now embedded in his heart or what his feelings for her were about to make him do.

He took her hands and rubbed his thumbs softly across the backs of her hands. They didn't have much time before the other ship reached them, so he needed to go with his gut. "If you think you can remove it, Shreya, I will trust you."

Chapter Twenty-One

Vox lay on the hard platform in the ship's small medical treatment room, his gaze fixed on the dark ceiling. He could hear Shreya moving around, pulling things from the cabinets as she searched for supplies. She'd declared the medical setup basic but workable, which did not increase his confidence.

"This is more like a repair than a surgery," she said as she bustled around him. "And I always liked tinkering with things as a child."

He did not like the idea of her tinkering with the implant embedded in his head, but he also knew he didn't have a better option. "Why did you not decide to become a doctor?"

"Something minor." She cleared her throat. "I sometimes get a little lightheaded at the sight of blood."

He bolted upright. "Minor? You might faint during the surgery?"

She pushed him back down with one palm on his chest. "It's been a long time since I fainted. I'm sure I've outgrown that phase."

"I think the escape pod might be a better option for me."

"Floating alone in space waiting to be picked up by the Kronock is better?" she asked, inspecting a handheld device from one of the alien med kits. Shreya pressed a button and a green beam shot out, scorching the corner of the countertop. She yelped and put it down.

"I may have better odds out there."

She gave him a side-eye look. "I told you. I'm not going to leave you to be tortured or turned back into one of them. Not if I can save you."

He clasped her wrist. "What if I am beyond saving?"

"But you're not." She smiled down at him, tracing a finger down the side of his face. "You've shown me the good in you."

"You really think I can return to life as a Drexian?" He heard the desperation in his own voice.

She nodded. "Of course. You're going to love the Boat."

He pulled her hand to his mouth, kissing her open palm. "And I can stay with you?"

Pink tinged her cheeks. "If you want, although I don't live on the fancy side with the holographic suites."

"I don't need fancy if I have you." He inhaled the scent of her skin and felt the trill of her pulse as he held her wrist.

Vox was acutely aware of the risk he was taking and wondered if this would be the last time he touched her. So much could go wrong. The chances of her being able to successfully and safely disable a sophisticated piece of cybernetic tech were slim, even as smart as she was. And if she did manage to remove it or render it inoperable, the Kronock might still track them down before they reached Drexian space. If that happened, he would have to surrender Shreya to them, or die trying to fight them off.

He sat up again, swinging his legs over the side and nestling her between them.

"What are you doing? I'm supposed to be prepping you for surgery."

"Soon." He pulled her close, tucking her head under his chin and inhaling deeply, memorizing the sweet smell of her hair. He ran his hands down her back until he reached the curve of her ass, his cock stirring.

Vox needed to imprint everything about her in his brain, but what he really needed was to claim her again. Once was not enough. He needed to convince himself she was really his, feel her body respond to his and banish the doubts swirling in his mind. Heat coiled in his belly as he remembered the feel of her tight heat sheathing him.

"Vox?" She tried to wiggle out of his grasp, but he held her in place with his legs. "This is really not making things go faster."

"You prefer it fast?" He slid his hands along the layers of fabric covering her legs, pulling the dress up until it was balled into his fists at her waist.

She slapped at him playfully. "You know that's not what I meant."

He lifted her in the air so she had to bend her knees to straddle his lap. Her pupils flared when he rested her on his hard cock.

"You're a very bad patient, you know that?" she said, her words soft and her hands gripping his shoulders.

"That is okay. I think you might like bad."

Shreya made a small sound of outrage. "If you're accusing me of liking bad boys, you couldn't be more wrong."

"No?" He unfastened his own pants, shoving them down and freeing his cock. "I thought you liked me."

She glanced at the hard length of him jutting up, and her tongue wet her bottom lip. "I do like you, but you aren't bad."

"But I've done bad things." He slowly lifted the dress completely over her head, tossing it on the floor. Vox cupped her breasts and thumbed her nipples. "I abducted you and tied you up and forced you to let me touch you."

A shiver went through her. "I like the way you touch me."

He could see that as the flesh around her nipples pebbled.

She lowered her voice to a whisper. "And if you really are a bad boy, then you're *my* bad boy."

Vox felt a surge of possession. He was hers, and she was his. No one could take her from him. He wouldn't let them. "You do not still want to escape from me?"

"I'm trying to save you," she said, taking his face in her hands. "So I can have more of this."

She lowered her mouth to his, her lips gently caressing and the tip of her tongue teasing. Her soft breasts pressed against his chest as she leaned forward, but he was so distracted by the taste of her mouth and the hardness of her nipples grazing his skin that he was startled when he felt her notch the crown of his cock at her opening. She sank down hard, and he let out a loud moan, his eyes rolling back in his head.

She matched his moan with a breathy one of her own as she moved up and down. His hands fell to her hips, his fingers biting into her skin.

Shreya pulled away, her face still so close he could feel her breath. She locked eyes with him, her gaze burning as she moved slowly. He felt lost in her eyes and in her exquisite tightness. Vox tried to steady himself, but his heart raced as his cock strained for more.

"You want it harder, don't you?" she asked. "You want to fuck me harder and faster."

He grunted. "I will go as slow as you want me to, mate."

She leaned close to his ear. "Tell me what you want, Vox."

He looped a hand around her waist and lifted her, flipping her onto her back in a single, swift motion as he thrust his cock deeper in her. "I want to hear you scream."

Her eyes were huge as she stared up at him, but her lips were curled into a smile. "Make me scream for you, Vox."

He drove into her hard, feeling her hands grasping his back and scraping along his nodes. Her touch on his hard bumps sent jolts of pleasure coursing through him, his senses scrambled. The only thing mooring him to reality was the sound of her cries as he thrust into her again and again.

Her jagged moans and hoarse screams urged him on, and when she began to convulse around him, her tight heat spasming around his cock and her body jerking, it was all he could do to hold on.

"Tell me you are mine, mate," he said, driving into her. "No one else can fuck you. Tell me this is only for me."

She arched her head back, panting as she hooked one leg around his waist.

"Shreya, answer me." He thrust deeply. "Mine?"

"Yes, Vox," she rasped. "Only yours."

With that, he exploded, holding himself deep as he pulsed hot inside her. Her arms shook as she clung to his back, breathing as if she'd run a race. He sank down next to her on the platform and braced himself on one arm so he wouldn't crush her.

She smiled up at him, her expression dazed, as the ship lurched to one side, and Cerise's scream pierced the air.

Chapter Twenty-Two

Shreya braced on hand against the curved walls of the ship's central compartment as she and Vox ran toward the cockpit, and the ship lurched again. What was happening? It didn't feel like they were being fired upon, but something clearly wasn't right.

Her stomach roiled, partly from the jostling of the ship and partly from fear. If the Kronock had found them, it was all over. She would be taken to a lab, and Vox would be pumped full of more Kronock DNA, at least until it finally killed him.

Bursting into the cockpit, she scanned the view out the front of the ship, only vaguely aware that Cerise sat in the pilot's chair. Her shoulders drooped when she saw the fleet of ships massed in front of them.

"Not Kronock," Vox said from behind her, although he didn't sound relieved.

"It's the Drexians." Shreya leaning against the back of a chair as she recognized the sleek black hulls of the ships. She glanced down at Cerise. "Is this why you screamed?"

"How was I supposed to know these were the good guys?" The alien flopped back in the seat. "One thrum we were flying, and the next thrum these ships materialized in front of us. Before I could do anything, they locked a tractor beam on us."

That explained the lurching. Shreya patted the alien on the shoulder. "It's okay. I'm just glad it isn't the Kronock."

The pilot's console beeped and a purple light blinked. Cerise squinted at it. "I think it's an incoming transmission."

"Let's hear it," Shreya said, straightening the dress she'd thrown over her head, inside-out.

Cerise pressed the light, and a static filled the small space, followed by a familiar voice.

"This is Dakar of the Drexian Empire. Identify yourself."

"It's me," Shreya yelled, hoping her voice was automatically transmitted and she didn't need to hold down a button or something, since she couldn't decipher the Kronock markings on the dark console. "Shreya."

Dakar let out a heavy breath. "Thank the gods—"

"Shreya?" Ella's voice cut him off. "Is that really you?"

Shreya put a hand over her mouth to keep from bursting into tears. Not only had the Drexians come looking for her, her friend was with them. She shouldn't be surprised Ella had managed to talk her way onto the rescue mission. It was exactly the type of friend Ella was—fiercely loyal and incredibly stubborn.

When she'd swallowed the urge to cry and taken a steadying breath, Shreya laughed. "Yes, it's really me. I can't believe you convinced the Drexians to take you on another bloody rescue mission."

"Can't you?" Dakar said, making Shreya laugh again.

"Why wouldn't they?" Ella asked. "Just because the first one was a total disaster?"

"Something like that," Shreya said. It was so good to hear her friend's voice and fall back into their easy banter. "How did you all find me? I don't have my tracker anymore."

"We know," another voice—deeper and more serious—came on the line. "Commander Dorn here. We suspected the hybrid would know to remove your tracker. Luckily, my brother still has contacts on Lymora III. He got a message that a Drexian cyborg has been spotted taking a human female to one of the famous pleasure houses."

Ella's voice broke it. "Shreya, are you okay? Did that monster do anything to you? If he did, I'll rip his—"

"I'm fine," Shreya insisted, glancing back to see Vox listening in the corner, his face a mask devoid of emotion. "Vox didn't hurt me. Actually, he saved me from the Kronock and the Xakden."

"Xakden?" Dakar sounded startled. "He fought off a Xakden?"

"Two, actually," Shreya said. "I'm glad you didn't go all the way to Lymora III to look for me."

"We were en route there, when our long range scanners picked up your vessel," Dorn said. "It seemed unusual to have a Drexian, human, and Perogling in a Kronock ship."

Shreya dropped her gaze to Cerise. "We were trying to get away from the Kronock and back to the Boat."

"I'm assuming the hybrid is restrained or sedated," Dakar said, more a statement than a question.

Shreya looked back at Vox, but he'd slipped out of the cockpit. "Actually, he's not. He isn't dangerous."

"Shreya," Ella said, her voice urgent. "He abducted you and took you to a planet that, from what I hear, is exactly where you want to take someone when you don't want them to be found."

Shreya recalled the straps on the bed and the apparatus hanging in the corner of the room. "At first, he was scary, but the more Drexian he became, the less dangerous he was."

"What do you mean, 'the more Drexian he became'?" Dorn asked.

"He hasn't had his regular injections to stabilize his Kronock DNA, which means it's weakening. He's literally becoming his old Drexian self again. Of course, this also means he needs medical treatment right away."

"We have your equipment and injections with us," Dakar said. "In case we were able to capture him."

She let out a breath. "Good. That will help a lot with the pains in his implant."

"We're going to tractor you into us and lock your ship beneath ours so we can come on board safely," Dorn said. "You're sure the hybrid won't put up a fight?"

"I'm sure. He agreed to come back to the Boat with me." She hesitated. "You have to promise not to treat him like a criminal. I told him he'd be able to return to life as a Drexian warrior."

There was a long pause before Dorn came back on the line. "You should not have told him that."

"Why not? None of this was his fault." Her voice rose a few octaves. "He was taken captive and tortured, then he was brainwashed and mutilated. You can't blame him for that."

"Shreya," Ella's said. "He kidnapped you. Why are you defending him? Is he making you say these things? Does he have a blaster to your head?"

"Of course not. He would never hurt me." Shreya's frustration rose like bile in her throat. "He's not dangerous. I promise."

"Then I promise you we'll treat him fairly," Dakar said over murmuring in the background.

"Prepare to be boarded. Commander Dorn out."

Cerise looked up at her with unblinking eyes, but Shreya couldn't meet them. Her new friend looked as worried as she felt.

"I need to talk to Vox." Shreya spun on her heel, heading out of the cockpit and running smack into him. She staggered back a few steps and he caught her by the arms. "Oh, I thought you were in the back."

He shook his head, his eyes downcast. "I heard everything."

She took his hands and squeezed them. "They don't understand because they don't know you yet. I promise you, everything will be fine once we explain it all."

"They are right." His voice sounded almost as toneless as when she'd first encountered him. "I did dishonorable things."

"But you also did a lot of really honorable things, like saving Cerise and me from those awful Xakden, and getting Cerise away from Zylia."

"They won't let me have you." It wasn't a question.

She didn't want to lie to him. "Probably not at first. You're going to be busy with medical treatments to get you back to normal. I'm sure once that's over, they'll take what you want into consideration. The Drexians are pretty big on matching warriors with humans. The last warrior who was rescued from the Kronock was given a tribute bride right away."

"I do not want a tribute bride." He stroked the backs of her hands and pulled her closer to him. "I want you. Only you. Isn't that what you want, too?"

"Yes, of course it is—"

The ship shuddered as something clamped on to it from above. Vox's gaze instinctively went up, then back to her, as he tightened his grip on her hands. "I cannot survive without you."

"I'm not going to leave you," she said. "I'll be with you every step of the way."

He lifted her face to his and crushed his mouth to hers, kissing her desperately as the ships locked together, metal scraping loudly against metal. Desire stormed through her, as his hands tangled in her hair, pulling her deeper into the kiss.

"Promise me," his words were short gasps when he released her. "Promise me you won't let them take you from me." His eyes raked over her face, taking in every bit of her as if he were seeing her for the last time. "Tell me you're mine."

"Vox, you know I am."

He nodded, kissing her forehead, then her cheeks and finally giving her a final kiss on the lips accompanied by a small sigh.

The steel hatch above them groaned as the mechanism was wrenched open from the outside. Vox stepped away from her, getting into a warrior's stance as Commander Dorn dropped down into a crouch, his blaster pointing squarely at Vox's chest.

Chapter Twenty-Three

Vox's finger tingled, aching to reach for his blaster, but the last thing he wanted was for Shreya to get hurt.

"I told you he's not the enemy," Shreya said, throwing her own hands up as the Drexian commander held his blaster steady, and another warrior dropped through the hatch beside him.

Vox recognized the second Drexian from the battle at the research facility. He'd stepped over him as he'd escaped, and remembered that the warrior had been more concerned with his injured crewmate than in giving chase.

"You okay?" the second Drexian asked, giving Shreya a questioning glance.

"I'm fine, Dakar." She exhaled loudly. "Vox is the one who saved me. He's the reason we're here."

"After he abducted you," Dakar reminded her, but his words weren't harsh. He walked over to Shreya, putting a hand on her arm and lowering his voice. "Ella has been going out of her mind since you were taken."

Vox eyed the interaction and felt a twinge of jealousy. How did she know this warrior well enough that he could touch her? Without thinking, Vox took a step toward her, a low growl building in his throat.

"Hold it right there," the Commander ordered, waving him away from Shreya. "Don't get any closer to the human."

The human? Shreya wasn't just any human. She was his mate.

"It's okay," Shreya said. "I promise he has no intention of hurting me."

"She looks unharmed, Dorn." Dakar turned and gave her a longer look up and down. "A little less like a scientist than the last time I saw you, perhaps."

She gave a weary laugh. "It's been a long few days."

"Is she okay, babe?" A female voice drifted down from the other side of the hatch.

Dakar grinned at Shreya, jerking a thumb toward the opening in the hull above them. "I wouldn't let her jump down until I knew the situation."

"I'll bet Ella loved that," Shreya said.

"She's fine," he called up. "All in one piece."

Dark, wavy hair spilled down from the open hatch, followed by a face as the woman leaned her head into the ship. "Seriously? That's all I get after flying halfway across the galaxy? 'All in one piece'?"

She saw Shreya, her eyes widening slightly, then her gaze fell on Vox and they popped open.

The Commander cleared his throat, his attention turning to Shreya. "We need to get the hybrid onto our ship so you can stabilize him. Are you ready?"

Vox flinched at hearing himself referred to as a hybrid, but he was comforted by the fact that Shreya would be treating him.

Shreya nodded. "Let me just get Cerise."

"I'm here," the tiny alien said, slinking out of the dim corridor and standing close to Shreya.

If the Drexians were startled by the presence of the Perogling, or by her opulent attire, they didn't let on.

"She's coming with us back to the Boat?" Dorn asked. "Because we aren't anywhere near her home world."

Shreya glanced at Cerise, who nodded vigorously. "Yep. I wouldn't be here without Cerise. She's going to be my guest on the Boat."

Dakar gave her a small bow and a wide smile. "A pleasure to meet you, Lady Cerise."

Cerise giggled, and Ella groaned from above.

"All right, Romeo," Ella said with a shake of her head. "Let's get cracking."

A pain spiked through Vox's head and he clutched his temple, listing to one side. Shreya reached for him, but Dorn blocked her.

"Step back," he said, keeping his weapon trained on Vox.

Even through the haze of pain, Vox knew he needed Shreya near him. They didn't understand, he thought. They didn't know she was his mate, and he couldn't be separated from her.

"Mine," he choked out the words as he attempted to push Dorn aside to get to Shreya.

Ella yelped from above and Dakar leapt for him, sweeping his arms behind him and forcing him to the floor. He struggled, even though the pain tearing through his temples made his limbs sluggish.

"Don't hurt him!" Shreya's cry sounded muffled, as if she was a great distance away. Her voice was muddled, with deeper voices yelling out commands, and even the high-pitched scream of the Perogling.

He bellowed her name and reared up, but the weight on his back was too great. Sinking back down, he flailed until his arms were spent and sweat beaded his brow. Vox felt something cold and hard clamp around his wrists, the metal biting into his skin.

"He's secure," the voice above him said, and the weight on his back lifted.

Vox was able to take a full breath, even though his head throbbed and his body screamed in protest. He twisted his head. Where was Shreya? Had they taken her away? Why wasn't she by his side? Hadn't she promised not to leave him?

"Is he hurt?" her voice was a choked sob, making his anger flare.

They'd made her cry. He struggled to move. He would make them pay for that.

"You will not take her from me," he said, lifting his head to meet Dakar's eyes. "She is mine."

Dakar tilted his head, as if studying him. "No, but he's pretty agitated." His gaze shifted to Shreya. "Does it have anything to do with why he grabbed his head?"

"Maybe," Shreya said, her matter-of-fact voice comforting. "He's been having worse and worse pains, which is why he needs treatment ASAP."

"Get him up," Dorn ordered. "We need him conscious to climb the ladder up into our ship. We'll sedate him once he's on board."

Vox felt himself lifted by his arms, the round center of the Kronock ship coming into focus again. He saw Shreya and Cerise both staring at him, concern etched on their faces.

He was desperate to reach out to Shreya, to touch her and let her know that everything was fine. He was fine.

"Shreya," he said, the word a desperate plea. He needed her to reassure him that things would not change between them once they returned to the Boat. He needed to know what he'd felt was real, that they were real.

"It's going to be okay, Vox," she said, her eyebrows pinched together. "We're going to get you all fixed up."

"Tell them," he said, looking back over his shoulder as Dakar marched him toward the open hatch. "Tell them you're mine."

Her eyes flickered, and her cheeks flushed. He felt Dakar hesitate, and saw Cerise glance quickly up at Shreya.

"He thinks she's still his captive." Dorn's voice was a dark rumble behind him.

Vox shook his head. "Not my captive. My mate."

The ship went quiet, then the woman hanging down into the ship laughed. "That's a good one. It would explain the clothes, although Cerise may be wearing the craziest bridesmaid dress I've ever seen."

Shreya laughed nervously, her gaze dropping.

"What's a bridesmaid?" Cerise asked her.

"He's delusional," Dakar said under his breath. "The DNA collapse must be affecting his brain."

"No, no, no." Vox fought to twist around and catch Shreya's eyes. "Tell them I have claimed you. Tell them."

Dakar sighed deeply as he struggled to keep Vox from lunging across the ship to reach her. "So much for waiting to sedate him."

The jab in his neck gave way to a serene darkness, and Vox sank into oblivion, relief mingling with fear.

Chapter Twenty-Four

Shreya paced a tight circle in the airy corridor, her footsteps echoing off the curved walls.

"You're going to wear a hole in the floor," Cerise said. "The doctors said the surgery might take a while."

Shreya looked down at the alien, who'd changed from her fluffy dress and wore a simple, blue shift that she suspected might have originated as someone's tunic. Although her clothes were less dramatic, her towering bouffant and brightly painted face remained unchanged. "What if the injections I gave him weren't enough?"

"I'm sure they were," Cerise said. "Didn't you say you're a scientist?"

"Sort of," Shreya mumbled. "I was taken from Earth while I was still at university—school."

"Whatever you did made it so Vox was able to reach the station. Now it's up to the medical team to do their bit."

Shreya nodded. On the trip back to the Boat, she'd given Vox the injections she'd formulated to stabilize his DNA, but she worried it wasn't enough. They hadn't been able to use their jump technology to speed the trip for fear it would damage Vox's already-fragile system, and every minute had felt torturously slow, even though they flew at near light speed.

He hadn't regained consciousness once since Dakar had sedated him, which meant she hadn't been able to apologize for not backing him up. She knew why she'd been reluctant to admit what had gone on between them. The Drexians would think he'd forced her, and Ella would think she'd lost her mind to sleep with her kidnapper. Even she didn't know why it felt so right when everything about them being together seemed like a bad idea.

She'd only been able to give him the injections and monitor his vital signs, sitting beside his bed for the entire trip and hoping he'd wake up. Cerise was right about one thing. The injections had seemed to stabilize him enough for him to make it back without any further reactions.

Commander Dorn had transmitted ahead, so a medical team had been waiting for them in the hangar deck, whisking Vox away before she even had a chance to kiss him goodbye. Removing the cybernetic implant and its ability to control him was deemed a top priority, and a team of doctors—as well as an medical AI that Dorn assured her was very skilled, if a bit arrogant—now worked to safely extract it from Vox's head.

Shreya choked back a sob. "What if he dies? They've never removed an implant like that."

Cerise reached up and put a tiny hand on her arm. "He seemed pretty strong to me. I'm sure he'll pull through."

Shreya pressed a hand to her mouth and nodded. She didn't know why she was so emotional over a man she'd only met a few days earlier—one who'd abducted her, no less.

The doors swished open, and a human with long, brown hair and a small, protruding belly emerged. Her gaze found Shreya and she smiled. "You must be the independent Dorn told me about." She held out a hand. "I'm Mandy, Dorn's wife."

Shreya registered that the woman was a tribute bride, and also seemed to be pregnant and in pink scrubs. "Are you a doctor?"

Mandy laughed and shook her head. "I wish. No, I'm learning, though. I work in the medical bay as an assistant. I heard you were waiting outside, so I thought I'd bring you an update."

Shreya's breath hitched in her chest. "How is he?"

Mandy smiled. "They were able to remove almost all of the device. The only thing remaining is a strip of metal near his temple, which they've left so his body can adapt to the change more easily. But the ocular implant is out and they severed the connections to his brain stem. He can no longer be controlled by the Kronock."

Shreya released the breath she didn't know she'd been holding. "Will he be blind in that eye?"

"Believe it or not, his real eye was underneath all that metal. There's a decent amount of scar tissue on his face and in his brain, which will take a while to heal, but he's going to be fine."

Shreya threw her arms around the startled woman, squeezing her tightly. "Thank you."

When she pulled back, Mandy cocked her head at her. "Dorn says you were abducted by this guy and held captive in an alien brothel."

"Where she met me," Cerise said, brightly.

Shreya's face warmed. She knew Mandy's implied question. Why was she so happy they'd saved someone who'd done all those awful things to her? She wasn't sure she could explain it herself.

"It's a long story," she said, hoping that was answer enough.

Mandy gave her a quick wink and rubbed a hand over her belly. "I've got one of those, too."

As the tribute bride spun around to return to the medical bay, Shreya called out, "When can I see him?"

Mandy hesitated in the doorway, glancing inside then back out. "They're wheeling him into a recovery pod as we speak. If you promise not to excite him, you can come now."

Shreya glanced down to ask Cerise to wait for her, but the alien already had her hands up. "Don't worry. I'll wait for you out here."

Shreya leaned down and gave her a quick hug. "Thanks. I promise to show you around the station properly, as soon as I see Vox with my own eyes."

Cerise waved her away, and Shreya followed Mandy through the arched doors. The space was wide and open, with a row of hovering beds running along the far wall. Metal arms extended from the high ceiling, and staff in white lab coats bustled around. Waist-high robots zoomed across the floor delivering trays of equipment and medicine, and Shreya paused to let one whiz past her.

She walked close behind Mandy to the side of the open space, passing through a doorway that led to individual pods, each one with transparent doors. Her breath caught in her throat when she spotted Vox lying on a bed in the first one.

Mandy paused outside. "These are healing pods used after surgery. The Drexians pump in pure oxygen, as well as healing compounds, so I can't let you stay long." She lowered her voice to conspiratorial whisper. "But you'll feel amazing once you leave."

Shreya barely registered the woman's words, as she opened the door for her and let her step inside. She was too focused on the changed Drexian, lying there with his eyes closed. Where the bulky, metal device had once covered nearly half of his face, now only a slim curve of metal arched from above his brow to the top of his cheekbone. The skin around the metal looked pink and fresh, with slight puckering.

It seemed strange to see Vox with an eyelid where a blinking red light had been. As frightening as she'd first found that pulsing light, it now felt odd to see him without it.

She fought the urge to touch him as she stood beside his bed, even though the bronze skin on his arms had scant few scaly patches anymore. She suspected it would be back to normal soon, and she breathed a sigh of relief that the injections seemed to have worked. She'd have to wait for additional testing, of course, but it was reassuring to know he was well on the way to being fully Drexian again.

She wondered if he would regain his former Drexian personality. She'd only known him as a part Drexian, part Kronock, part cyborg hybrid, so she was curious how different he would seem to her when he was fully Drexian. Her heart beat faster at the thought of being with this huge, gorgeous creature.

It might take some serious explaining, and perhaps pulling a few strings with the Drexian High Command, but she couldn't wait to live with him on the station. Not as a tribute bride, but maybe in officer's quarters like her friend Ella.

He stirred, and her pulse fluttered with excitement.

"Vox. It's me, Shreya. I'm right here, just like I promised. I never left you."

His eyes opened, and for the first time she saw them both—that startling, beautiful shade of sea green. He blinked slowly, as if testing them out. "Shreya?"

She leaned closer. "The surgery was a success. You're going to be fine. Everything's going to be fine."

He squinted up, his gaze drifting around the room. "Where am I?"

"You're on the Boat. We got you back here, and the doctors were able to remove the implant." She rested her fingertips lightly on the sheet pulled across his waist.

"The Boat?"

"The space station I told you about. The place where you and I are going to live together." She laughed. "As soon as I explain everything to the Drexians."

"Shreya," he said her name slowly, like he was saying it for the first time. He took in her face, his brow wrinkling. "I'm sorry, but I don't know who you are."

Chapter Twenty-Five

Vox gazed up at the pretty human standing by his bed. Her eyes swam with tears, but he did not know why.

"Are you a doctor?" he asked.

He could tell by the sterile surroundings that he was in a medical bay of some kind, and the groggy feeling in his head backed up his assumption. The air held a sharp, astringent scent, reminding him instantly of every medical bay he'd ever visited.

"No." Her voice shook as she spoke, and she pulled her hand back from the sheet tucked around his bare chest. "I'm...don't you remember me?"

"I'm sorry." He raised a hand to the side of his head, which was tender to the touch. "My memories are jumbled. You said I'm on a space station?"

She nodded, her dark eyes seeming to search his. "A Drexian space station. Do you remember that you're Drexian?"

He couldn't help chuckling a bit. "Well, of course I remember that. I'm Vox of House Kalaff."

She tilted her head at him. "What's the last thing you remember before waking up?"

He concentrated on thinking back. "I was on an intelligence mission deep in Kronock space. I found a deserted planet where they were building ships, but ships like we've never seen the Kronock build before. I remember trying to send a transmission, and fearing that I'd revealed my location." He sat up higher in the bed. "I need to tell High Command about the Kronock technology."

"That's it?" she asked. "Nothing after that?"

He closed his eyes for a second and remembered something more. "I was trying to outrun a Kronock fighter when I was hit. I must have crashed, but how was I recovered in Kronock space?"

The woman pressed her lips together before giving him a small smile. "I'm glad you survived. That's all that really matters." She took a step back. "I'm going to let one of the Drexians explain everything to you."

He wanted to ask her more, like why she looked familiar when he knew he'd never laid eyes on an Earth female before, but she was gone.

Vox let his head flop back on the pillow. His head ached, and strange images flashed through his mind. He instinctively rubbed his arms, jerking his hand back when his fingers brushed something scaly.

What was on his skin? He picked at one of the raised, gray scales and flinched when he realized it was part of him.

"I wouldn't do that unless you want holes in your arm."

Vox raised his eyes to the broad Drexian warrior stepping into the room. From his uniform, he knew the warrior was a commander, but the long hair told him he was part of Inferno Force. He lifted an arm to his chest in salute.

The warrior saluted back. "I'm Commander Dorn."

"Vox of House Kalaff."

"So you remember?" Dorn said, rocking back on his heels.

"My name? Why wouldn't I?"

Dorn clasped his hands behind his back. "You had an invasive surgery to remove a cybernetic implant from your head. Since it was connected to your brain stem, the medical team suspected there might be memory loss."

Vox's fingers flew to the metal strip curled around one temple and his stomach tightened. "A cybernetic implant? I don't remember that."

"No? Do you recall being captured by the Kronock?"

"Captured?" His mouth went dry. "Impossible. The Kronock don't take prisoners."

The commander shrugged one shoulder. "Not routinely, no. Recently, our enemy has changed its behavior."

Vox nodded, remembering what he'd wanted to tell someone in charge. "Yes. That's what I was trying to tell High Command when I was leaving Kronock space. They're building new ships, massive ships, like nothing we've ever seen before, especially from them."

Dorn did not seem surprised.

"I saw an entire planet they'd turned into a massive factory to turn out ships," Vox continued. "They've got technology we've never seen from them before, sir."

"Oh, we've seen it," Dorn told him.

"I don't understand." Vox narrowed his eyes and glanced past the warrior and out the clear door. "How could you have seen them? I'm in military intelligence, and I know we haven't seen anything like that before. Is this really a Drexian space station or is this some hallucination, because nothing I've seen or heard makes sense?"

"I'm no hallucination," Dorn said.

"Then why do I have scales on my arm and metal in my head? How can you know about the Kronock ships I saw for the first time just a few days ago, and why did a human come talk to me about living on the Boat?"

Dorn sighed deeply. "It's been more than a few days. You've been missing for… a while."

Vox started at this revelation, shaking his head. *Impossible.*

"As I said before, you were taken captive by the Kronock." The commander held a hand up when Vox started to protest. "They experimented on you, injecting you with their DNA in order to make you more like them. It worked for a while and you became a kind of cyborg Drexian-Kronock hybrid."

Bile rose in Vox's throat as he stared at Dorn. He didn't know what Drexian commander would make up such a wild tale, but how did he not remember any of this?

"At some point they outfitted you with one of their cybernetic ocular implants, I'm assuming so they could control you more easily, although we know from records we obtained that they also tortured and brainwashed you."

Vox cringed as he remembered a jolt of pain and a harsh voice repeating phrases in his ear. "I was on a mission."

Dorn's gaze was steady. "Their plan was to use you to destroy both us and Earth."

Vox's palms were clammy, and he dragged them up and down the sheet. "How could I help destroy Earth?"

"Their general, whom my brother killed in an explosion, thought if he could successfully merge Kronock DNA with human, he could use that to spread his race throughout the planet. Once they'd invaded, of course."

Vox remembered an explosion, and he also remembered a general. Krav. A chill went through him as the gnarled Kronock face flashed into his brain. "They needed a human, but Krav had failed. They needed me to take a human."

"Which you did when we arrived at the research facility to rescue you," Dorn said. "Luckily, your body was already starting to reject the Kronock DNA, so you became more and more Drexian. When we finally tracked you down, your body had almost shut down. If it wasn't for Shreya and her ability to stabilize your DNA, you would have died before we reached the station."

"Shreya," Vox said. "The human who was in here before you. That's how I know her. She saved me?"

"She saved you, but that's not how you know her. She's the human you abducted as part of the Kronock plan.

Vox felt like he'd been punched in the gut. He'd abducted a woman? "I don't remember that."

"Probably for the best," Dorn said.

Vox's face burned with shame. No wonder the woman had been so confused when he didn't know her. "I didn't hurt her, did I?"

The Drexian commander's eyes dropped. "She claims you didn't, but she has not be forthcoming about what did actually happen on Lymora III."

"Lymora III?" His voice was a hoarse croak. "Why would I take her to that depravity-fueled planet?"

Dorn shrugged. "When we intercepted your ship, you were

carrying a Perogling pleasurer, and Shreya wore what looked like a Valoushe dress."

"How…long?"

"How long were you gone? Approximately six months."

Vox felt the blood rush from his face. All that time lost…What had he done? What dishonorable things…?" He scraped a hand roughly through his hair. Most importantly, he suspected he owed the pretty human an apology, although he wasn't sure for just how much he needed to ask her forgiveness.

Chapter Twenty-Six

Shreya slumped in the low-backed chair in her suite while Cerise bustled about the room, opening and closing cabinet doors.

"You must have something to drink in here," the Perogling said, standing on her tiptoes to open the doors to the wardrobe and then closing them again.

Shreya shook her head. "Not really. I don't usually do a lot of drinking in my room."

"There's a first time for everything, honey."

"I can't believe he doesn't remember any of it," Shreya said. "I'd understand if he forgot a few things, or some of the details, but to forget everything that's happened to him since he was taken by the Kronock...?"

"They did have to do major surgery on him," Cerise reminded her. "And the thing they removed was attached to his brain. He's lucky he didn't end up catatonic, or permanently damaged."

Shreya knew Cerise was right. She should be grateful he'd survived the surgery and hadn't suffered massive brain damage or paralysis. Especially since he'd been in pretty bad shape when they'd gotten him to the station.

Vox not remembering anything that had gone on between them wasn't something she'd even contemplated. She'd been more worried about the fallout of them being together, or what would happen to him once he returned to the station, since he'd technically committed multiple crimes against his own people. But this? She never thought she could have been wiped from his memory.

A hard knot churned in her stomach as she thought about the blank look on his face when he'd gazed up at her. It was like he wasn't even the same person she'd known. Part of him had been removed—the part that had stolen her heart.

Cerise rested a small hand on her shoulder. "He might get his memory back."

"But the doctors can't say for sure if he will. They've never removed a cybernetic implant from a Drexian brain before. It's entirely possible he never remembers anything he did while he was under Kronock control, or anything that happened."

Cerise hopped up into the chair across from Shreya, her legs dangling nearly a foot off the floor. "That might not be such a bad thing. It sounds like he did things he wouldn't be proud of."

Shreya swallowed hard wondering if she was one of those things he would regret having done. "I feel like I've been ghosted and gaslighted. Did anything I remember really happen?"

Cerise giggled behind her hand. "As someone who heard a lot of what happened, I can tell you that you weren't imagining it."

Shreya's cheeks warmed. "And he doesn't remember any of it. I guess I don't have to be afraid of him thinking I was too wild."

"That's not wild," Cerise said. "You should hear Bulgarvi mating calls."

Before Shreya could hear more than she probably wanted to about alien mating calls, a series of taps came from the door, followed by a beeping that let them know someone was on the other side. With a sigh, she stood and crossed to the door, swiping a hand over the panel to open it.

"There you are," Ella said, striding into the room with their friend, True, behind her. She held a bottle of something pink, and a paper bag. "We've been looking everywhere for you. Mandy said you left the medical bay an hour ago. I thought you might be on the promenade, showing Cerise around."

Shreya gave Cerise an apologetic look. "Not yet. I promised her I'd give her a full tour tomorrow. We're both pretty wiped out after the trip back."

True slipped an arm around Shreya's waist and gave her a quick hug. "We're all so relieved you're okay. I knew Ella wouldn't give up, but when they said you were abducted by a cyborg, I was so scared for you."

Shreya return the blonde's hug. "Actually he wasn't a cyborg. He was a Kronock-Drexian hybrid, with a cybernetic implant."

True laughed. "Okay, that did not make him sound less scary."

"By the time we intercepted his ship, he was in a pretty weakened state," Ella said. "He was babbling a lot of crazy stuff, but he didn't seem dangerous."

"He never hurt me," Shreya said. "And he saved us from some pretty terrifying Xakden."

True shuddered. "Do I want to know what a Xakden is?"

"Definitely not," Cerise said.

True smiled at her and held out a hand. "You must be the woman who escaped with Shreya."

"That's me," Cerise smiled brightly. "The day Vox walked into the pleasure house was my lucky day."

True's eyes grew wide. "Pleasure house?"

"It's not as bad as it sounds," Shreya told her, knowing how easily shocked True was. The pretty blonde had grown up in a very religious family, and was not what you'd call worldly, especially when it came to men.

"Well, we're celebrating you getting out of there, even if it wasn't so bad, and finally being back on the boat with all of us other independents," Ella said, twisting the cap off the bottle.

Shreya pulled several glasses out from underneath a cabinet, and put them on the coffee table. "I heard you aren't an independent anymore. I heard you moved in with the Dakar on the officers' side of the station."

Ella waved her hand as she poured four glasses of the pink, fizzy liquid. "I'll always be an independent at heart. You know that. But it is nice to be able to be with Dakar."

Shreya accepted the glass Ella held out to her, feeling a lump grow in her throat. She tossed back the contents as Ella was raising her glass to make a toast.

"Okay, then," Ella said, eyeing Shreya and reaching for the bottle to refill her glass. When she poured a new one, Ella tilted her head at her. "Are you sure you're fine? Is there something you aren't telling us?"

Shreya shook her head, but she couldn't speak, the tears welling up in her eyes and making her blink quickly. "It's Vox. He's forgotten me."

Ella set her glass on the table without drinking it. "I heard Mandy say he lost all the memories of being with the Kronock and basically having been one of them."

"Considering the fact that he was tortured and did a bunch of awful things," True said. "Don't you think it's better for him not to remember?"

Shreya pressed the backs of her hands against her eyes. "I know I should want him to forget all of that, but if he forgets everything that happened, then he forgets everything that happened with me."

She didn't remove her hands from her eyes, but she felt the room go still.

"What happened with you?" Ella asked

Shreya let out a long breath. "I think I fell in love with him. And he said he wanted to be with me. Our plan was to be matched and live together on the boat."

"Holy shit," Ella said. "You fell for the guy who abducted you?"

"I know it sounds crazy, but he changed." Shreya dropped her hands from her face and saw everyone gaping at her, except for Cerise. "The more Drexian he became, the more I saw who he really was underneath the cybernetic implant and the scaly bits."

Ella rubbed a hand over her face. "How close did the two of you get?"

"Pretty close," Shreya said, her cheeks warming.

"So you and Vox…?" True prodded, her eyes wide.

Shreya nodded.

"More than once," Cerise added with a giggle.

Ella picked up her drink and took a large gulp. "And now he has no memory of any of it, and you still have feelings for him?"

"Of course I do," Shreya said. "Bloody hell. I didn't want to fall for the guy, believe me, but I did, and I can't make myself forget it all in a snap."

True came over and stood behind her, wrapping her arms around Shreya's shoulders and giving her a squeeze. "No one expects you to, but what are you going to do if he never remembers?"

Shreya shook her head slowly. "I don't know. I guess I'll have to get over it ,then. It's not like I'm even a tribute bride who could ask to be matched with him. I'm an independent, and I made it pretty clear in the past that I didn't want to participate in any part of the tribute bride program."

"I was in the same boat with Dakar, and look at me now," Ella said. "Anything is possible."

"But you had a guy who knew who you were." Shreya's breath hitched in her chest. "Mine doesn't even remember my name."

Ella started pacing across the room. "Then you need to make him remember you."

Shreya looked up. "How?"

"Maybe his memory loss is like amnesia, and memories can be triggered by seeing or hearing familiar things," Ella said. "You need to spend time with him, and remind him of things you experienced together."

Shreya bit the edge of her thumbnail. How could she trigger Vox's memory, when most of their shared experiences had been on a lawless planet, and in an alien brothel? She couldn't exactly bring in a Xakden for him to fight, or install a giant X-cross in her room. She shuddered at the thought of both of those. Not even if she'd wanted to, which she didn't.

"Didn't you tell me this station is partly holographic?" Cerise asked, sipping the drink that was a nearly identical match to her hair.

Ella snapped her fingers, beaming at the alien. "Why didn't I think of that? Cerise, you're a genius."

Shreya looked at Ella and Cerise grinning at each other. "Why do I have the feeling I'm going to regret this?"

Chapter Twenty-Seven

Vox raked a hand through his hair as he exited the chamber of the High Command. He'd been drilled so long he'd lost track of time, but one glance at the dimly lit corridors told him it was late.

Commander Dorn came out of the room behind him and clapped a heavy hand on his shoulder. "You did well in there."

"I didn't have the answers they wanted."

Dorn shrugged. "You can't tell them what you don't remember."

"All those things they said I did…" He let his words trail off, not sure if he could give voice to his question.

"It wasn't you," Dakar said, emerging from the High Command chamber and joining them in the hall. "It was the creature they made you into."

Vox put a hand to his head, flinching when he touched cool metal. "Apparently, I still carry traces of that creature."

"The doctors will remove that last part once you've healed a bit more," Dorn said. "My mate tried to explain it to me. Something about the scar tissue that had formed around the implant and not wanting to shock your system too much by removing everything at once."

"I thought maybe it was to mark me as a former traitor," Vox said.

"We all know you were a victim of the Kronock," Dakar said, his expression earnest. "We all read the documents outlining what they did to you."

"I recall flashes of pain and a Kronock voice, but little else," Vox told them. "I wish I could tell you and the High Command something more useful."

"There's a possibility that the Kronock designed the implant to destroy your memories if it was removed," Dorn said. "My mate went into more detail about it, but to be honest with you, I didn't understand half of what she said."

Dorn motioned for them to start walking down the corridor and the Drexians fell in step with him.

"She is the one who attended me in the medical bay?" Vox asked, remembering the woman with long, brown hair and the protruding belly. "The one who is…"

Dorn nodded, a grin spreading across his face. "Pregnant? Yes, although she refuses to stop working." He frowned. "She claims Earth females do not lie around during their pregnancies."

"She brought another female to see me," Vox said. "The one I abducted."

Dakar exchanged a glance with Dorn. "Shreya. She worked with us to develop the injections that stabilized your DNA. She's the reason you're alive."

Dorn swiped a hand in front of the inclinator panel, and they stepped into a sleek compartment with pulsing lavender light.

162

Vox swallowed hard as the inclinator dropped down and then rotated to the side. The station was so different from the Drexian battleships and outposts he was used to, and he found the bright lights and soft colors unsettling. Everything on the Boat smelled too good, or felt too smooth, or was too quiet. Even the music piped in everywhere made him nervous. Where were the sounds of battle, the smell of burning fuel, and the wide expanses of dark metal that he knew to be Drexian?

The doors swished open, and Dorn led the way down another corridor. Vox was too weary to ask where they were going, but he hoped it was someplace that had food or drinks.

When another set of wide double doors slid open, Vox's shoulders eased. Instead of white surfaces and colored illuminations, this large space was lit only by glowing candles on the small, dark tables and down the long ebony bar. Black carpet covered the floor, and extended to the floor-to-ceiling window that took up the entire far wall and looked out into space.

"Where are we?" he asked.

"The officers' club," Dakar told him. "Looks blessedly different from the rest of the station, no?"

The Drexian didn't wait for an answer as he steered Vox over to the long bar, nodding to the heavy-set, purple-skinned bartender, and ordering three Noovian whiskeys.

A Drexian already at the bar turned and greeted them. "That took long enough."

"Sorry we made you wait, Zayn," Dorn said. "The High Command had a lot of questions."

The new Drexian—Zayn, from what Dorn had said—gave Dorn a quick fist-to-chest salute, and Vox noticed scars across his forearms. He turned to Vox and smiled. "I'm Zayn. The commander thought I might be a good friend for you to have on the station, since I've been through some of what you have, as well."

Vox studied the man, but saw no evidence of an implant.

Zayn must have noticed his gaze and shook his head. "The Kronock didn't give me an implant like yours, but I was their captive and endured their torture. The implant they put in my head wasn't visible, but it caused a lot of damage to the station."

"But it's gone now?" Vox asked.

Zayn grimaced. "Yes, but the process wasn't pleasant."

"And your memories?"

"Unfortunately, I still remember everything." A dark look passed across his face. "I think you might be lucky not to remember."

Vox nodded, but he wasn't sure if he agreed. Knowing that so much time had been wiped from his brain made him feel like he was missing a limb. Even if it had been painful, he thought he'd rather know than feel like a part of his life was a black hole.

Dakar raised his glass to toast. "To lost comrades who have returned."

They all clinked their glasses before slamming back the contents. Vox winced as the bitter liquid seared his throat, but he welcomed the heat in his belly. At least it took away the numbness that had engulfed him since he'd awoken.

Vox tapped the rim of his glass for another, and the thick-jowled bartender poured him another shot of the green whiskey.

"You don't remember a thing about your time with the Kronock?" Zayn asked him, leaning closer and lowering his voice. Vox suspected he didn't want to advertise that they'd both spent time with their enemy. Dorn and Dakar had turned toward each other and were discussing the latest Inferno Force news, giving the two Drexians time to talk privately.

Vox searched his mind, coming up with only a few garbled sounds and swirling images. "Nothing concrete. A voice, but no words that would be helpful. Flashes of pain."

Zayn nodded. "The pain doesn't go away so easily."

Vox dropped his eyes to the Drexian's arms. "From the Kronock?"

Another nod. "I kept these as a reminder."

Vox touched his fingers to the metal curving around his temple. "I suppose I have a reminder, as well. Even though I have almost no memories, I have this."

"You seem upset that your memories are gone," Zayn said. "Why?"

Vox rotated the cool glass in his hand, swishing the green liquid. "What if I'm responsible for the death of others, or for the destruction of entire planets? With the Kronock, I have no idea how they could have used me, and it makes me ill to think I may have done things to hurt others. I need to know what I've done so I can make amends."

"I get that," Zayn said.

"Apparently I abducted a human female, but when I met her, she didn't seem to be angry with me. She was more upset I didn't remember her name."

Zayn leaned his arms against the bar. "Your memory loss must have been a shock to her."

"I need to apologize to her." Vox took a gulp of whiskey. "Although I am not sure how much I need to apologize for. Did I hurt her? Did I threaten her?" He dropped his head into his hands. "As a Drexian, I would have never done any of those things, but as a Kronock. . ."

Zayn put a hand on Vox's back. "Human females are more resilient and forgiving than you'd think."

"Do you know much about humans?"

"A little." Zayn grinned. "I have an Earth mate who continues to impress me with her intelligence and cunning."

Vox raised an eyebrow. "They gave you a tribute bride after you returned from being a Kronock captive?"

The corner of Zayn's mouth twitched up. "She was my reward for escaping from the enemy. Perhaps they will reward you, as well."

Something niggled in the back of Vox's brain. Something about tribute brides. He reached for the memory, but it slipped away like smoke.

"Maybe," he said, although something in him resisted the thought.

Vox didn't know much about himself at the moment, but he knew without a doubt that he did not want a tribute bride. Now he needed to figure out why.

Chapter Twenty-Eight

"This is a bad idea," Shreya said, as she watched Cerise run around the holodeck. Standing at the door, she marveled at just how much the space looked like the suite in the pleasure house on Lymora III—gilded mirrors, red fabric draping from the gold, four-poster bed, and all.

"The bed was a bit bigger," Cerise said, then raised her voice. "Computer, increase bed size by ten percent."

The bed grew in size, and Shreya had to tell herself that it was not the bed where she'd been tied up, no matter how much it might look like it.

Ella stood next to her with her hands on her hips. "So this is where you were taken when Vox abducted you?"

"Pretty much." Shreya made sure not to let her eyes wander over to the hanging apparatus and the giant X on the far wall. "Not that he used… I mean, we didn't do…"

"Oh, I know," Ella said, waving a hand. "I'm sure all the rooms in an alien brothel look like this."

"They do?" The startled expression had not left True's face since

167

Cerise had started recreating the suite, and she twirled a strand of her blonde hair nervously as she eyed the straps on the bed.

"Not all of them," Cerise said as she flounced over, her hair bobbing. "Some of the rooms in the house were really kinky."

The twist of hair fell from True's finger. "This isn't considered really kinky?"

Cerise giggled. "Not at all. There isn't a single whip on the wall."

Shreya turned to face Ella. "Thanks again for pulling some strings to get us access. I know independents aren't supposed to use the holodecks on the tribute side of the station."

Ella gave her arm a quick squeeze. "You can thank Dakar for arranging it, but I don't think anyone would have refused you after everything you did to save Vox *and* after you were kidnapped in the process."

"Do you think this will work?" Shreya asked.

"I honestly don't know. If seeing familiar settings can trigger memories then I don't see why being in a recreated suite where you two spent time wouldn't shake something loose, but…"

"But he might have more than a simple case of amnesia," Shreya said. "If removing the implant actually damaged the part of his brain that stored the memories, then nothing will bring them back."

"And there's no way to know which it is," Ella added with a reassuring smile, "so trying this is probably your best bet for getting him to remember."

"I hope so." Shreya took a few steps into the room, eying the low table in the middle. "Computer, decrease table size by twenty percent."

The table shrunk, and she nodded. That was better. She glanced at the table of liquor bottles in one corner. "There was a bottle of green booze."

"Noovian whiskey," Cerise said quickly.

"Computer, add a bottle of Noovian whiskey to the liquor selection." Shreya said, remembering how much of the whiskey Vox had drunk.

Cerise fluffed a velvet pillow and tossed it onto one of the chairs. "I think it's ready. Are you?"

Shreya hesitated as she looked at the carefully crafted setting. What was she doing? Did she really think Vox would walk into the holodeck, see the suite, and his memories of her would come flooding back? Maybe. The bigger possibility was that he'd walk in, not have any idea what was going on, and think she was delusional.

"Shreya?" Ella shook her shoulder. "Are you sure you want us to leave?"

"I can stay outside the holodeck in case she needs me," Cerise said. "I was part of the original experience, so it wouldn't jolt him out of the memory."

"You don't think this whole setup will make him flash back to being one of the Kronock?" True asked. "There's no chance he could remember the wrong things, is there?"

Shreya hadn't thought of that, and her stomach tightened at the thought of Vox reverting back to the hybrid version, who was so hell-bent on his mission.

"Impossible," Ella said, sounding way more confident than Shreya felt. "The Kronock DNA has been removed, as well as the implant that connected him to them. Most of it, at least. The Drexians wouldn't let him walk around the Boat if they thought there was even a remote chance of him switching back."

"And if he does, I'll take care of it," Cerise said, pulling a blaster out of her pocket.

"Where did you get that?" True asked, starting to swirl a strand of hair on the other side of her head.

Cerise shrugged. "I slip in and out of places easily. No one notices me if I don't want them to."

Shreya's gaze went to the bubble-gum-pink wig, and wondered how that went unnoticed anywhere, but she didn't say anything. "I don't think it will come to that, but I appreciate knowing you have my back."

Cerise winked at her. "I've set it to stun, honey. Don't want to damage that hunk too much, now do we?"

Ella raised her eyebrows at Shreya and gave her arm a final squeeze, as she looped an arm through True's and headed for the holodeck door. "Well, we'd better get out of here before Vox arrives."

Cerise gave her a wave with the blaster as she followed them out. "I'll be right out here if you need anything."

The double doors swished shut, and Shreya was left in the recreated pleasure house suite by herself. She knew Dakar had agreed to bring Vox to the holodeck, and she hoped they weren't delayed. Her nerves wouldn't survive much of a wait.

She crossed to the drink cart and poured two glasses of Noovian whiskey, her eyes trained on the door. Any minute now, she thought, as she walked the drinks to the low table and set them down.

She rubbed her clammy palms on her thighs. Should she be sitting on the bed when he walked in? She swallowed hard. Should she be laying on it? Should she be tied up?

No. She shook her head vigorously. That was too much. Looking down at the green whiskey, she picked up one of the glasses and took a sip. The sharp taste made her shudder as it scorched her throat, but she felt her nerves begin to calm. Before she could decide whether or not to take another sip—or perhaps knock back the entire drink—the doors opened, and Vox walked in.

He stopped when he saw her and tilted his head. "You."

She concentrated on lowering the glass to the table without dropping it. "Shreya," she reminded him.

"Of course. Shreya. I remember from the medical bay."

She bit back her disappointment that the medical bay was still his only memory of her. She swept an arm wide. "Do you remember any of this?"

Vox wrinkled his forehead as he pivoted to take in the suite, his face registering surprise when he reached the apparatuses in the corner. "Should I?"

Shreya felt tears threaten the backs of her eyes, but she forced herself to breathe deeply. Don't rush it, she told herself. He's only been in here for a minute.

"This was the room we stayed in on Lymora III," she told him.

His eyes returned to the giant X, and his gaze went to the floor. "I hope one of those drinks is for me."

"Yes," she stammered, picking them both up and handing one to him. "I know you like Noovian whiskey."

He took a long gulp, wincing as he swallowed. "You seem to know more about me than I know about you."

"You used to know things about me," she said, trying hard not to sound accusatory, but feeling childish, nonetheless.

He stared into his glass. "I'm sorry I don't remember. The doctors say the removal of the implant could have removed all my memories from the time it was put in."

"So you remember before then?"

He nodded. "The torture and brainwashing is hazy, but it's coming back to me in pieces. Unfortunately."

She studied the face she thought she'd known—the square jaw and soft lips—and saw the pain behind his eyes that hadn't been there before. Remembering had to be as painful for him as his not remembering was for her. Did she really want to push him to remember things that would cause him even more pain and regret? Even though she was glad of the way things had turned out, she doubted he'd be proud of how he'd behaved when he'd been focused on his mission.

"I'm sorry," she said. "That must not be fun."

He shrugged and downed the last of his whiskey. "It's nothing I don't deserve."

She took a step closer to him. "You can't blame yourself for things you did when you were being controlled by the Kronock."

He gave a brusque shake of his head. "That's the problem. I don't know everything I did." He waved a hand at the room. "I have no idea what happened here, although I don't know if I want to know."

She looked at the shaking hand clutching the glass and let out a breath. "Nothing happened here."

He jerked his head up. "Really?"

She forced herself to smile. "Nothing you need to be ashamed about, at least."

His gaze scoured her face. "Are you sure? If I hurt you, I need to make amends."

Shreya shook her head. "I promise you didn't hurt me. I mean, you did when you knocked me out and dragged me off my ship, but I don't remember that, so we'll say it doesn't count."

He let out a breath that was almost a choked sob as he pulled her into a hug. "You don't know how relieved I am to hear that. I don't know if I would have been able to live with myself if I'd violated my Drexian honor." He pulled her away and held her at arm's length. "Or yours."

Her heart hammered so loudly she was sure he could hear it. His touch had felt so good, even if it had only been a hug. She wanted more. Much more. She gazed into his eyes, searching for that flicker of recognition. That spark of desire that had been there before. But it was gone. He didn't remember.

Shreya backed away from him, her throat constricting as she did.

"Are you okay?" he asked, his relief fading as he looked at her.

"Fine," she lied. "The whiskey might have gone to my head."

He motioned to the chair. "You should sit." He glanced back at the bed. "Or lie down."

She couldn't even look at the bed now without feeling sick. "No, I should be getting back to my side of the station."

He walked toward her. "Before you go, I want to thank you. I hear I owe you a debt of gratitude for keeping me alive until I reached the station."

"You're welcome." Shreya swiped a hand to open the doors. She needed to get out of there before she broke down and made a fool of herself.

"And I owe you an apology—for knocking you out and abducting you, for taking you to a planet like Lymora III, for putting you in danger." His gaze darted around the room. "For frightening you."

She steadied herself as she turned back and took a final look at him. "Thank you for the apology, but all those things were worth it."

"Worth it?" He looked confused.

"You were worth it, Vox," she said, her voice soft and trembling.

She spun on her heel and ran, not stopping when he called out to her, or slowing down when she heard Cerise's voice through the haze of tears blinding her way. Instead, she stumbled down the corridor more quickly, away from the warrior she loved.

Chapter Twenty-Nine

Vox trudged back to his officers' quarters, not noticing the stream of aliens passing him in the wide corridors, or the cacophony of chatter that filled the air. His mind was stuck on the look Shreya had given him before she'd left the holodeck.

He was no expert on females, but it did not seem like the look you gave someone who'd been your captor. There was something more there, something pleading in her eyes, but he didn't know what she wanted.

Dragging a hand across his forehead, he rounded a corner and slammed into another warrior, stumbling back as he tried to right himself. "My apologies," he said, relieved when he saw it was someone he knew.

"No worries," Dakar said, picking the tablet he'd been carrying up off the floor. "I wasn't watching where I was going."

"No," Vox said. "I'm to blame. I was distracted."

Dakar studied him for a beat. "You sure you're okay?" He lowered his voice and glanced around them. "The Boat can be a tricky place to adjust to. Everyone says it's the greatest place ever, but it's not, if you're used to war-worn battleships and grimy outposts."

Vox released a breath. "It doesn't feel like anything I've known."

Dakar put an arm around his shoulders. "I felt the exact same way after coming here from Inferno Force. The last thing I wanted was a place that was too clean, had too many rules, and not enough available females."

Vox cocked an eyebrow at him as a group of giggling tribute brides passed them. "Not enough females?"

Dakar moved them down the corridor. "Not enough *available* females. I was used to the pleasure planets, but here all the tribute brides are spoken for. Of course, I ended up with a mate from the independent side of the station, but that's pretty frowned upon."

"Independent?" That rang a bell of familiarity in Vox's memory. "Shreya said she was an independent."

Dakar nodded as they walked. "She's friends with my mate. They both rejected the whole tribute bride concept and went to live on the other side of the station. There aren't many of them, but there are more than the Drexian High Command would like to admit."

"So Shreya does not want a Drexian mate?" Vox asked, not knowing why this answer felt so important to him.

"I can't speak for her, but she didn't go for the idea when she was first taken from Earth and brought here. Of course, my mate didn't, either. She was the most fiercely independent one of them all." Dakar grinned. "Until she met me."

"So they can change their minds?"

Dakar eyed him. "Keeping human females happy is the entire purpose for the Boat, so they have more power than they think. Why do you ask? Did you and Shreya…?"

"No." Vox shook his head. "I mean, I don't think so. She claims I have nothing to apologize for. But I don't have any memories of her, so I can't be sure."

Dakar let out a low whistle. "You don't remember a thing about that entire time on Lymora III? Now even fighting off the Xakden?"

"I fought off Xakden?" Vox strained to pull up a memory of that, but there was nothing.

"According to Shreya and her little friend, you killed two of the *grekking* aliens, and saved the females from a pretty nasty fate."

The idea of Shreya being in danger from two Xakden made something stir inside Vox. It must have been his natural Drexian instinct to defend and protect, he thought, as his heart beat faster.

"And nothing from the pleasure house?" Dakar waggled his eyebrows at him. "I've never been myself, but I hear the Valoushe's place is something of a palace, with just about any female alien you could desire."

Vox shrugged. "I only know what our room looked like. At least, from the replica Shreya created on the holodeck for me."

Dakar stopped short, and a pair of Drexian warriors nearly ran into them. "She recreated the room where you held her captive?"

Vox's face warmed. "I think she was trying to help bring back my memories, but it didn't work. I have no memories of being in a place like that."

"Why would she care so much about you remembering?"

Vox shrugged. "I do not know. I suppose she is trying to help, since she was so involved in saving my life."

Dakar nodded, but didn't look convinced as he resumed walking.

"In my experience, females do not do things without a good reason."

Vox recognized the doors in front of them. They led to the officers' quarters, where his room was located. He glanced over at Dakar, as the warrior swiped a hand to open the doors. "Do you live here, as well? I thought you took a mate? Don't all the mated Drexians lived in the holographic suites?"

Dakar gave him a crooked grin. "I told you my mate was fiercely independent. She didn't want to live with the other tribute brides, so we opted to stay in my suite on the officer's deck. It caused less uproar than me moving into the independent wing would have."

Vox followed the warrior down the narrower corridor, stopping when he recognized his door. "This is me."

Dakar jerked a thumb at the door across the hall. "And that's me. Well, Ella and me." He thumped Vox on the back. "Feel free to come over anytime if you need something."

"Thank you." Vox gave him a small bow before passing his hand over the panel beside the door and watching Dakar do the same behind him. He heard a female's voice inside Dakar's quarters, before the door slid shut behind him and blocked out the sound.

Stepping into his own suite, Vox was overwhelmed by the silence. Not only the silence of the empty room, but the silence in his own head. He had scant few memories of the implant that had been in his head, but he felt the loss of the voices he knew had been projected into him. Even though the idea of Kronock voices in his head horrified him, he couldn't stop the feeling of loneliness that now engulfed him.

Vox crossed the dimly lit room to the window that stretched across one long wall. The view of space was spectacular, but the vast blackness dotted with stars made him feel even more alone. He pressed one palm against the cool glass, noticing that the skin on his arms was smooth and bronze. Patches of scales no longer marred the surface.

His gaze drifted to his reflection in the glass. The only evidence that remained at all was the curve of metal around one temple. Once that was removed, there would be no way to tell he'd ever been part Kronock, or part cyborg. He would know, of course. He'd always carry the guilt of not knowing what he'd done when he was under the enemy's influence.

He slammed his hand on the glass. Why couldn't he remember? Had the implant really taken all his memories with him, or was he suppressing them, because they were so horrific his psyche couldn't handle it?

Grek. He was a Drexian warrior. He'd been trained to handle extreme duress. It was how he'd survived the torture he occasionally recalled, his mind bringing up his own screams and then pushing them away again.

Vox crossed to the large bed, sinking onto the ebony duvet. He flopped back, letting himself sink into the softness and closing his eyes.

Think, he ordered his mind. *What happened on Lymora III?*

He pictured the room Shreya had created on the holodeck, flinching at its gaudiness and obvious purpose. He'd visited pleasure planets before, of course. All Drexians had. But he'd never seen a room like *that* one. His face warmed as he thought of the giant X with the straps at the corners.

He pressed his eyes together as he concentrated, trying to bring up images of himself in that room. After a moment, he let out an exasperated breath and relaxed. Nothing.

Maybe Shreya had been telling the truth and there was nothing to tell, although the knot in his stomach disagreed with him. As he lay sprawled out on the bed, he heard a pinging from the door. He opened one eye. There it was again.

Standing, Vox crossed to the door and swiped a hand to open it. His gaze dropped to the tiny alien with a tower of pink hair, and shimmering skin that held a faint blue hue. She'd changed into a ridiculously ornate dress, with piles of ruffles belling out from her waist.

"I thought you might be hungry," she said, pushing a levitating cart into the room.

He blinked a few times, not sure if he was imagining things.

The alien beamed up at him as she removed domes from plates of food. "These are a few of the things you enjoyed on Lymora III. I thought you might enjoy them here."

Vox was about to protest that he wasn't hungry and didn't want Lymoran food, when he inhaled the scent of sugar. Although Drexians didn't consume many sweet foods, he recognized the aroma and it made him salivate.

"You should try the cream," the Perogling said, pointing to a plate piled high with something fluffy and white as she backed out of the room. "It's something Shreya concocted for you."

Before he could ask why Shreya would have created a dish for him, the alien was gone.

Vox shook his head as he approached the food. There was nothing he recognized, although the sweet scent did feel familiar. He inhaled deeply and closed his eyes, feeling warmth spread throughout his body. Opening his eyes again, he leaned closer to the plate of fluff the alien had called cream. He'd never heard of cream before, and couldn't imagine why the human would have made it for him.

He touched the top of it, startled by how airy and cool it was. The feel of it on his fingertip sent tingles down his arm.

Vox brought his finger to his lips and sampled the odd substance. It was the sweetest thing he'd ever tasted, but that wasn't what made him almost lightheaded. He closed his eyes again and took another scoop of cream, sucking it off his fingers slowly and remembering the taste of Shreya's fingers in his mouth.

He'd been sitting on the edge of the bed and she had been feeding the sweet, fluffy cream to him. As he swallowed, he could almost feel her skin between his lips, the bumpy flesh beneath his tongue. The pebbled skin of her nipples, not her fingers, he realized, his knees nearly buckling.

He scooped more cream into his mouth, the taste bringing up visions of Shreya in a diaphanous white dress that he slowly untied, revealing the perfect mounds of her breasts. He could hear her breathy moans as he sucked her, her skin sweeter than any cream he could imagine.

Blood rushed south, and his cock throbbed. How had he not remembered until now? He heaved in deep breaths as all the memories flooded his brain—watching Shreya shower, dressing her as she was tied to the crossed beams, licking cream off her breast, and taking her up against the wall of the ship, her eyes dark as she told him she was his.

His head pounded as he staggered toward the door. He needed to find her. He didn't know what he would say, but he knew one thing for sure. She was his.

Chapter Thirty

Shreya lay facedown on her bed. She'd cried herself out, and now felt weary from her grief. As unbelievable as it seemed, he didn't remember her or anything that had happened between them, and she needed to accept it and move on.

Easier said than done.

She pushed herself up and swung her feet over the side of the bed. She wanted to curl up in a ball until she didn't feel an ache in her heart every time she thought about Vox, but that wouldn't do anyone any good. Neither would drinking herself into oblivion.

Yanking a hand through her hair, she squared her shoulders. Work had always gotten her through hard times before. When she'd lost her family, she'd thrown herself into her studies. It hadn't made everything better, but it had made it easy not to think about how much it hurt.

That was what she needed now, she reminded herself. To dull the pain of loss. Focusing on the research she'd been doing before the mission to rescue Vox would provide exactly the distraction she needed to forget about him.

Shreya stood, appraising herself quickly in her dresser mirror and wiping the tears off her face. Running her fingers through her hair to smooth it, she looked around for her messenger bag, scooping it off the floor next to her dresser and heading for the door. She hadn't been back to the lab since she'd returned to the station, and she hoped her station hadn't been poached by other scientists.

She strode out of her suite and down the corridor, passing the independent coffee shop and waving at the silver-haired alien lazily wiping the bar. She could tell it was late at night by the low lighting and by the fact that almost no women occupied the high-top tables or overstuffed couch.

Good, she thought. I'll have the lab to myself. Unless some of the night owl alien scientists were there.

Passing through the sliding double doors that divided the independent section from the rest of the station, Shreya walked briskly down the corridors. The piped-in music was barely audible—another clue it was late—and few aliens were out and about.

She stepped onto an empty inclinator, grateful not to run into anyone she knew, or anyone she needed to make a point of ignoring, like the ever-flirty Neebix. At this point, she wasn't sure she trusted herself not to fall victim to their good looks and swishing tails.

When she reached the lab, she let out a deep breath. The long, high tables were almost completely empty. Only one purple-skinned alien sat on a hover stool, his webbed feet swinging beneath him as he peered into a microscope.

Shreya wound her way to the back of the lab and found her station. Breathing a sigh of relief when she realized nothing had been touched, she set down her bag and hopped onto her stool. Even her notes were exactly where she'd left them, and she scanned the top page to bring herself up to speed, flinching slightly when she read the notes outlining her hypothesis about Vox's DNA.

Pushing thoughts of the well-muscled Drexian out of her mind, she started writing down the results of administering her injections when Vox had been in transit to the Boat. As she'd hoped, the Drexian DNA had begun to overwrite the Kronock DNA, and had countered the negative effects of the DNA collapse.

Tapping her pen on the counter, she wondered if she could get the medical records of his surgery to add to her notes. For a moment she thought about submitting her research to a scientific journal until she remembered she was on an alien space station, and there were no scientific journals.

She laughed quietly to herself. She could fill an entire scientific journal just with descriptions of the Boat. Forget about her research. People on Earth would freak out at the thought of a holographic space station filled with alien creatures, where tables and carts hovered, and elevators went from side to side and diagonally, as well as up and down.

Dropping her pen on top of her notes, she leaned back. What next? She'd solved the issue with Vox's DNA. Now, she needed another project to keep her busy, and keep her mind off the hot Drexian she'd fallen for. She groaned with exasperation. Coming to the lab hadn't distracted her from thinking about Vox. Looking at her old notes about him had made her think about him even more.

Closing her eyes, she tried not to think about him, but images kept flashing in her mind—her hands running down the hard muscles of his chest, his tongue on her skin, his cock inside her.

Shreya shook her head. "You have to forget about him," she muttered.

"I hope you aren't talking about me."

Her eyes flew open, and she nearly slipped off the hovering stool. Vox stood only feet away from her, his face flushed and his eyes intense.

"What are you doing here?" she asked, grabbing the edge of the counter for balance.

"I've been looking for you all over the station." His breathing was ragged, and she wondered if he'd *run* all over the Boat. "The alien in the independent section finally told me you'd left with your work bag. Dakar told me where you went when you worked. Now here I am."

"I can see that." Shreya didn't know what else to say. When she'd left him only a couple of hours earlier, he'd had no memory of her. If he'd come to give her another polite apology or thank you, she didn't know if she could bear it. She took a deep breath. "If you've come to thank me again, don't. I was only doing what anyone would have done."

"I haven't come to thank you." He stepped closer to her, and his green eyes flashed dark.

She wondered if he was okay, since he looked a bit feverish. And, if she was being honest, a little possessed. "Are you having some side effects from the surgery? I'm not a doctor, but I could call one for you."

"No." He took another step toward her. "I do not need a doctor, Shreya."

The way he said her name made a shiver run down her spine. Her pulse quickened, and her mouth went dry. She stared up at him, as he closed the remaining distance between them. "What do you need, Vox?"

He leaned down so that his mouth brushed her ear. "I need you to tell me that you're mine."

Her entire body jerked, and she sucked in air. He grabbed her by the ass and lifted her off the stool, wrapping her legs around his waist.

Tears burned her eyelids, and she buried her head in his neck to keep from sobbing. "You remembered," she finally managed to whisper.

He nodded. "I remember everything. I'm so sorry it took me so long."

She leaned back, taking his face in her hands. "It doesn't matter. As long as you remember how mad I am for you."

He tilted his head at her. "Is being mad for me a good thing?"

She laughed. "A very good thing."

"Then I am very mad about you, as well," he said, before setting her down on the counter and crushing his mouth to hers.

Chapter Thirty-One

V ox heard little but the rush of blood thrumming in his ears as he kissed her, his tongue insistent as it tangled with hers. His memories of being with Shreya had come back in a rush, and now he felt that avalanche of sensation and emotion threaten to engulf him.

Pulling her into him, he leaned forward so his cock bumped up against her. She let out a small gasp, her hands clutching his back and rubbing up against his nodes. The jolt of pleasure that shot through him was enough to make his knees buckle.

How could he have forgotten this for even a second? She felt so right in his arms—the taste of her so intoxicating he could barely think straight. As need pounded through him, one thought dominated his mind. She was his. Only his. Always.

"Vox," the sound of her voice as she pulled away from him was soft and breathy.

He moved his hungry mouth down her neck, nipping her skin as he went and savoring the warm softness. "Mmhmm?"

She laughed and the vibration of her throat tickled his lips. "Vox. We should probably find a more appropriate place."

He lifted his head to meet her eyes, and saw her looking beyond him. Twisting around, he spotted a small, green alien on a hovering stool gaping at them through a pair of thick goggles.

"If we aren't careful, we might end up being studied," Shreya whispered.

"Can't have that." Vox lifted her ass off the table, her legs still wrapped around his waist, and started walking out of the lab.

"What are you doing?" she asked, her face warm as they passed the alien staring up at them with wide, magnified eyes.

"Taking you someplace more appropriate."

"Like this?"

"Why not?" Vox asked. "I can walk faster than you, and I find it enjoyable to feel you pressed up against me."

"I can tell." His hard cock bumping up against her left her in little doubt of just how enjoyable he found the position.

Luckily, the corridors were relatively empty and set to nighttime illumination, although they were still bright enough for the aliens and Drexian warriors who passed them to do a double-take.

When they stepped into an inclinator compartment, a Vexling with a lilac twist of hair remained outside, saying, "I'll take the next one."

The doors swished closed, and Shreya swatted at Vox's broad shoulders. "You terrified that poor Vexling."

Vox pressed her back against the inclinator wall as it surged diagonally upward. "If he was terrified by me carrying you, then it is good he chose to wait for the next compartment."

With that, he ground his hips up so that his hard length teased her through her pants. She let out an involuntary sigh before he captured her mouth in his, rocking his body into her as he stroked her tongue with his own.

Vox was only vaguely aware of the inclinator doors opening, but he was aware of the deep throat-clearing. Pulling his attention from Shreya, he glanced over to see Dakar standing outside the inclinator, the grin on his face wide.

"Looks like another independent might be joining us on the officers' wing," he said.

"Do not be surprised if neither of us emerges from my room for a very long time," Vox said, carrying Shreya past the Drexian warrior.

Shreya looked up at Vox, a dazed expression on her face. "Fine by me."

He stumbled down the corridor as Shreya nuzzled his neck, hearing Dakar chuckle behind him. Swiping a hand over the side panel, Vox hurried to open the door, bursting inside and staggering to the bed.

Shreya bounced a few times when he dropped her back on the soft surface. Her hair fanned out behind her on the ebony bed covers, and her eyes were half-lidded with desire.

Vox growled low. Desire arrowed through him as he looked at her splayed out beneath him. His female. His mate.

"Tell me you are mine, Shreya." He tugged roughly at the bottom of her pants, pulling until they were on the floor.

"You know I am," she said, wiggling her hips that now wore nothing but a small pair of pink panties.

He ripped her shirt open and buttons flew across the room. "Say you're mine."

Her breath was jagged, her breasts heaving under the matching pink lace of her bra. "I'm yours, Vox. I've always been yours."

He bent down, taking one nipple and sucking it through the rough lace, feeling it harden between his lips. She whimpered, and Vox thought he'd never heard a sweeter sound.

Clutching his shoulders, she arched her back as he moved to the other nipple, sucking it into his mouth and feeling the bumpy fabric over the pebbled flesh. He unhooked the front clasp, and her breasts sprang free. Vox cupped both globes in his hands, thumbing the nipples and watching Shreya writhe.

"So beautiful," he murmured, dipping his head to the space between her breasts and trailing kisses down her belly.

When her reached her panties, she inhaled sharply. Moving his hands down to slide her panties from her hips, Vox peered up at her. "Every part of you is beautiful, and every part of you is mine."

Her gaze became molten as he dragged her panties slowly down her legs and pulled them off entirely. His cock throbbed at the sight of the neat, narrow strip of short, dark hair. "Spread your legs for me."

She hesitated, staring at him through thick lashes. So she was still shy, he thought. He would need to coax her back to the point where she felt she could surrender to him.

Vox stood up, tugging his shirt over his head and dropping his own pants. He tossed them both on the floor and stood naked at the foot of the bed. Her eyes drifted to his rigid cock, and she grinned.

"Better?" he asked, loving the way her eyes devoured him.

She opened her mouth, as if to speak but closed it again when he lowered his head between her legs, which fell open. Running one finger through her hot folds, he found the nub between her legs and stroked it.

Shreya jerked, looping her legs around his back and dropping them open even more. He replaced his finger with his tongue and began sucking her, as she gasped and fisted her hands in the covers.

The taste of her was intoxicating, as were the urgent moves of her hips rising up to meet his mouth. He lavished her with his tongue, as he slid a finger into her tight heat, feeling her hips move faster.

"Vox," she panted.

He didn't stop flicking his tongue as he thrust a second finger inside of her, hearing her sharp gasp. She was so close, he could almost feel the fire coiled inside her.

He pulled back for a moment to catch a glimpse of her flushed face. She jerked her head up when he stopped. "Vox," she said, her words desperate gasps. "I need…"

He nodded, savoring the look of molten desire burning in her eyes. "You need me, Shreya."

"Yes, Vox. I need you. Please…"

He returned to her slick nub, sucking it as he pumped two thick fingers deep inside her. Within moments, she was trembling, her hands raking across his back and catching his nodes. He felt his own arousal surge as Shreya shattered, bucking and moaning and clawing at him. She knifed up with a final scream before collapsing on the bed.

His cock throbbing, Vox sat up on his knees, gazing down at his mate who lay with her eyelids fluttering and her light-brown cheeks flushed pink.

"Shreya," he said. "Spread your legs for me so I can claim you."

"You've already claimed me," she said, her voice little more than a whisper as she opened her eyes fully. "Don't you remember?"

"Of course I remember." He grabbed her ankles and held one in each hand. "But I can never claim you too many times, my beautiful mate."

Her eyes, which were already dark pools, became nearly black as she let her knees fall open. Vox slid his hands down to her hips, tilting her up and steadying his breathing as he notched his cock at her entrance.

Her breath caught in her throat as he pushed slowly into her, and he fought to keep his eyes from rolling into the back of his head. She felt amazing, her hot tightness gripping him like a vise.

"You feel so good," she said, moving her hips to take him deeper. "And so big."

Vox gritted his teeth to keep from exploding, leaning his head back as he drove his cock all the way to the hilt. *Grek*. She was so wet and tight.

"Vox," her voice teased him. "Don't you want to watch?"

He swallowed hard as he returned his gaze to her lush body, nearly choking when he saw her stretched tight around his cock. Gods. It took all his restraint not to pound into her, but he wanted to feel her release while he was inside her.

"So perfect where I split you," he said, his voice husky.

Her gaze followed his, and she smiled. "I've never liked watching myself get fucked before."

He groaned, fighting to keep himself from careening over the edge. Hearing his pretty, sweet mate talk like that made it almost impossible not to lose control. "Now you like to watch?"

She nodded, wetting her bottom lip with her tongue. "Your cock is so huge, and you stretch me so tight."

Grek. The woman was driving him to the edge. Vox bit his own lip until he tasted blood.

Shreya raised herself up on her arms, curling one hand round his neck and pulling him into a deep kiss. He dragged his cock out and thrust back in as her tongue fought with his. When she pulled away and moaned under her breath, he thrust hard and held her tight.

Shreya kept one hand around his neck as she shifted up onto his lap, her legs wrapped around his waist. "You shouldn't get to have all the fun."

As she moved herself up and down on his shaft, he reached down to where their bodies met, finding her slick nub and rubbing the pad of his thumb over it. Her tightness fluttered around him, and she threw her head back, her bucking hips chasing after her release.

When Vox stroked her wet nub harder, she shattered. Her limbs convulsed, her body gripping his cock like a fist. Vox's tenuous hold on his self-control snapped with a roar, as he spilled into her.

Shreya sank against him, her palms slipping as she dragged her hands down his chest, glistening slick with sweat. Her breath was warm as her face pressed into his heaving chest, and Vox kissed the top of her head, unable to form the words to speak.

"I don't remember *that*," she said, with a soft laugh.

"Nor do I." Vox shifted inside her, still hard, and she emitted a tiny yelp.

"Now, *that* I do remember. Drexians can keep going."

Vox felt his arousal stir again. "If you are ready, my insatiable mate."

"Mate." Shreya laughed and kissed the hollow of his neck, sending a shiver down his spine. "I like the sound of that."

Chapter Thirty-Two

Vox opened the clear-sided box on his bed and pulled out a stack of neatly folded clothes, setting them on the black covers.

"You're sure you're okay with sharing closet space?" Shreya asked, standing in front of the open wardrobe doors and inspecting the shelves. Even though there was not much inside, the space seemed scant for two people.

"I do not need much, aside from a couple of uniforms."

She cocked an eyebrow at him. "I hope you don't plan on wearing your Drexian military uniform when we're alone together."

"No? You would not find the authority arousing?"

Shreya's face warmed. "You don't need a uniform to get me turned on."

He picked up a stack of shirts and walked them over to her, nuzzling her neck as he came up behind her. "I am glad to hear it."

His warm breath on the nape of her neck sent a shiver of pleasure down her spine, and she swayed on the spot. "We're supposed to be moving me in, remember?"

"Of course I remember." He placed the stack of clothes on one of the bare shelves then reached around and cupped her breasts in his hands. "I promised you I would never forget again."

Sinking back into him, Shreya groaned. "At this rate, we'll never get me unpacked."

"That's okay." He thumbed her nipples through her blouse. "I like to take things slow."

Heat throbbed between her legs, and her nipples hardened. "The High Command gave us their approval three days ago."

"And it took two days for me to demonstrate my happiness to you," he murmured. "These things can't be rushed."

Shreya felt her core tighten as she remembered the last two luxuriously indulgent days where they hadn't left the bed for anything but food, often summoned by Vox in the middle of the night and delivered by a groggy Vexling.

"My friends are going to wonder what happened to me."

Vox took her earlobe between his lips and nibbled it lightly. "I doubt it. Your friends know we appealed to the Drexian High Command to be bonded. They must have heard the good news, and they know we would not have the bonding ceremony without them."

The thought that everyone knew exactly what they been doing for the past two days made Shreya's face warm even more. Damn the Drexian if he couldn't get her worked up with the slightest touch.

Before she could scold Vox for distracting her yet again, the door beeped.

"Ignore it," Vox muttered, tracing his tongue around the edge of her ear.

"It's probably the rest of my boxes." Shreya spun away from him, dancing out of his reach and dodging his attempts to pull her back in his arms, as she hurried to the door.

"She's alive," Cerise called out when the door glided open, bustling past her into the room, followed by a short alien with spiky, purple hair, and a Vexling with a swish of blue hair that made her easily six feet tall.

"Hey, Cerise," Shreya said, noticing that her friend wore a tiny three-piece suit in a shocking shade of green. "Sorry I've been a little hard to track down lately."

The woman bobbled her pink wig. "Don't worry. Ella and True helped me get a suite of my own in the independent section, and I got a job."

"A job?" For a moment Shreya wondered if her new job was anything remotely similar to her old job, although she was pretty sure they didn't encourage prostitutes on the Boat.

Cerise nodded vigorously. "You're looking at the newest tribute bride wedding liaison intern. I'm working with Reina and Serge."

Shreya glanced at the Vexling, who was shifting from one foot to the other and biting the edge of her thumbnail. "I didn't know they did internships on the station."

"We don't," the purple-haired alien in the banana-yellow suit said. "But Reina here is a soft touch." He extended a hand to her. "I'm Serge."

"I thought it couldn't hurt." The Vexling, who was obviously Reina, shrugged. "Besides, Cerise was instrumental in rescuing a human off of Lymora III."

Serge cleared his throat and glanced back at Vox. "Perhaps it's best not to dwell on Lymora III. All's well that ends well, I always say."

"Indeed." Vox came to stand behind Shreya, wrapping one well-muscled arm around her waist.

"I'm glad you're doing so well." Shreya tried to ignore the hard bulge pressing against her back as she smiled at Cerise. She gave her head a shake as she realized her friend was dressed almost identically to Serge—the only real difference being the color of their suits. "It sounds like you've been keeping busy."

"We're preparing for a new shipment of tribute brides, and Serge and Reina have been teaching me everything they know. I'm so excited I'll get to practice on your wedding."

"My wedding?" Shreya looked from one smiling and nodding alien to the other. "What do you mean, my wedding?"

Cerise's brow furrowed. "You are getting married, right?"

"Well, yes—" Shreya began.

"Then you have to have a wedding," Serge said, holding up a stubby finger. "And every decent wedding needs a wedding planner."

Shreya craned her head around to peer up at Vox, who wore an amused expression. "I didn't know independents got to have fancy weddings. Ella hasn't had one."

Serge threw up a hand. "Do not get me started on Ella. That child is dancing on my last nerve."

Shreya raised an eyebrow. "Dancing on your last nerve?"

"No one uses colorful Earth sayings like Serge," Reina said, beaming at him.

"I'll agree with that," Shreya said under her breath.

"There's a very good chance I get you down the aisle before I get Ella to decide on a theme for her wedding," Serge said.

Shreya felt her pulse quicken. "We need a theme?"

"A theme, leitmotif, color palette," Serge continued. "Perhaps we include your Earth heritage?"

"You want to have Vox enter on an elephant?" Shreya asked.

Serge's large eyes widened, as he rubbed his hands together. "Oh, yes!" He blinked a few times. "What's an elephant?"

Shreya laughed, and began to steer the aliens out of the suite. "Can we do this when I'm not so knackered? I promise to think about my theme if we can postpone until tomorrow."

Serge sighed as he allowed himself to be herded into the hall. "Fine, but don't forget."

"Don't forget," Cerise repeated, wagging a finger exactly like Serge was doing.

Shreya waved as she slid the door closed behind them, her shoulders sagging as she turned back to face Vox. "If I didn't know Cerise was a Perogling, I would swear she was morphing into a Gatazoid."

Vox chuckled. "Whatever she is, I owe her a debt of gratitude. If she hadn't fixed all that food to jog my memory, it might have taken much longer for me to remember."

Shreya felt a rush of warmth that the woman hadn't given up, even when she was convinced that Vox was a lost cause. "I think that earns her a place in our wedding."

"Maybe she should ride the elephant."

"You know," Shreya said. "She would probably love that. But weren't we in the middle of unpacking?"

"We were in the middle of something." Vox reached into the box on the bed and withdrew a black strip of fabric. "Is this what I think it is?"

Shreya's heart raced as she gave her mate a wicked smile. "I was hoping you'd find that. I saved it from Lymora III."

Vox walked toward her, holding the blindfold in one hand. "I'm afraid the wedding planner is going to be disappointed tomorrow, as well."

Epilogue

Captain Varden strode down the corridor, nodding at officers he passed. He was not in his uniform, but every Drexian on board knew who he was.

As the captain of the Boat, he commanded a sizable number of warriors, and was responsible for the defense of the Drexian's most valuable assets—the high-tech space station and the tribute brides aboard it. He took his responsibility seriously—even more so, after the attack by the Kronock and the sabotage engineered by them—and sometimes the constant stress ate away at him. He was grateful the rescue mission to recover one of their captive warriors and a human female had been successful, but he needed to *not* think about missions and battle strategy for a while.

Which is why I need this, he thought, pausing at the entrance to the recreational holodecks. He'd saved up his holodeck time so he could enjoy a serious workout with a Kranji master, and he was itching to practice the alien martial art he'd first learned at the Drexian Academy.

As with most Drexians, fighting calmed him, especially a discipline such as Kranji—considered by most to be the most challenging sport in the universe. Just thinking about it made his heart beat faster.

His fingers hovered over the control panel, but his eyes were drawn to the holodeck next to the one he'd reserved. A simulation was running, and he cocked his head to one side when he read the name on the panel.

Gulf of Mexico?

This was clearly not a Drexian program, and he assumed a Drexian was not running it. Drexian warriors favored battle recreations, or obstacle courses designed to test their strength and skill.

A tribute bride, he thought at first, eying the name on the panel under the simulation title. Then he shook his head. The name was human, although he realized it was not a tribute bride's. He prided himself on remembering every match made on his ship since he'd taken the helm, and this human had not taken a Drexian mate. Of that he was certain.

"True." He said the name out loud, liking the way it sounded.

If she wasn't a tribute bride, that meant she was one of the brides who'd rejected her mate. He felt a small flash of annoyance that any female would not want to be mated with one of his fellow warriors. He'd always felt the humans that were abducted from Earth were lucky to be taken from a planet fast on its way to destroying itself, and even luckier to be matched with a species as noble as the Drexians.

The fact that he'd never taken a tribute bride was no reflection on the program, or on humans. Unlike some on the Drexian home world, Varden had no issues with his people taking humans as mates, or with the half Drexian-half human babies that resulted. He found the Earth females attractive, as well, even though his contact with them was limited.

No, none of these things were the reason behind his lack of bride.

Simply put, he'd missed his window. When he'd been in his prime, he'd been a fourth son, and so far down the list his name had never come up. But all that time he'd been steadily moving up the leadership ladder, until he was finally appointed captain of the Boat.

Learning how to lead an operation as massive as the space station that housed thousands of aliens had absorbed every moment of his time, and before he realized it, he was no longer the young warrior he'd once been. His hair had gone prematurely gray at the temples, making people think he was older than he was, although his bronze skin was unlined and he was as muscular and fit as any of his officers—frequent Kranji practice ensured that. But his time-consuming job and few gray hairs reminded him that tribute brides and babies were not something that was in the cards for him. He'd quietly taken his name off the long list, and had never felt bitter about it.

Varden started to punch in the code for his Kranji program when the name on the other panel pulled him back. What did this Gulf of Mexico look like?

Curiosity got the better of him, and he punched in his captain's code so he could join the simulation in progress, knowing that it was technically speaking against protocol to do so. Once someone was in the holodeck, only an emergency override could allow someone else access. He'd never taken advantage of his authority before, but he felt an inexplicable desire to see the simulation.

Just a peek, he told himself.

The doors slid open silently, and he stepped inside, his mouth dropping open as he took in the scene stretched out before him. The Gulf of Mexico was more beautiful than anything he'd ever seen before. He stepped forward, realizing the ground under his feet was soft and his shoes were sinking into it. He took them off and left them by the door, his bare feet making imprints in the white, powdery substance as he walked toward the thing that captivated his attention.

Water extended out as far as he could see, bright and turquoise-blue as the fiery sun shone on it. Waves rolled in, cascading onto the ground in front of him and rushing up to his feet in a torrent of bubbles. The cool water felt bracing as it swirled around his toes, sucking the ground out from under him as it rushed backward.

Reaching down with one hand, he dipped his fingers into the water and tasted them, flinching from the saltiness.

"I wouldn't drink too much of that," a voice called out.

Varden spun around and saw a blonde woman walking toward him, wearing a pale-blue dress that was suspended from her shoulders by string ties and carrying a pair of flimsy shoes hooked over one finger.

"The salt water will just make you more thirsty," she said, "although I doubt that would matter, since you're not real."

He blinked at her. This must be True, one of the Earthlings who'd rejected being a tribute.

She waved a hand at him. "This has Ella written all over it."

"Ella?" he asked.

The blonde looked him up and down, even walking around him to get a better view. "The badass martial-arts outfit is a nice touch, considering she knows I have a thing for martial-arts movies."

He glanced down at the black Kranji uniform that crossed his chest and was belted at his waist.

"Did she make you left-handed?"

He held up his hands. "Left-handed?"

"Do you write with your right or your left hand?"

"Left," he said, wondering what the pretty human was babbling on about.

She closed her eyes for a beat and made a soft moaning noise. "Of course you do. I'm surprised Ella didn't make you look like a young Jean Claude Van Damme. Then I'd really be in trouble, although you're pretty hot yourself." She reached up on tiptoes and touched the hair at one of his temples. "I like the distinguished grays."

As breathtaking as the setting was, Varden was beginning to think he'd made a mistake sneaking into the simulation.

"So, what?" she asked, pushing her long, straight hair out of her face, as the breeze blew it forward. "Miss Computer Expert added you into my holodeck program because she thought I needed a man?"

Varden opened his mouth, but didn't know what to say. *Hi, I'm not a simulation. I'm actually the captain of the ship.* He instinctively knew she'd be humiliated by the reveal, so he decided to shrug.

True turned back toward the water. "Maybe she's right, although I think this has more to do with her being head-over-heels, and wanting everyone else to feel the same way, than me actually needing a guy."

He didn't say anything, but he watched her profile as she stared out at the water.

"It has been a lot quieter now that my best friend is living over on the officers' deck. I can't just pop into her suite in my PJs." She drew a line in the soft ground with her toe. "And now that Shreya is going over there, too, it does feel a little lonely."

Varden had never given much thought to the reject section of the station, although now he suspected it would feel isolating to be separated from the rest of the station. He felt a pang that this pretty human was lonely enough to strike up a conversation with what she thought was a computer-generated character.

True inhaled deeply, raising her arms over her head and stretching. "I know the stars are beautiful, but somehow they can never match the ocean for me."

"This is beautiful," he said.

She nodded. "We used to come here when I was a kid. At least, the Earth version of it." She bent and picked up a handful of the powdery substance covering the ground, letting it cascade through her fingers. "I remember playing in sand like this, and thinking it was the softest thing I'd ever touched."

Sand. The white stuff was called sand. Varden couldn't help but be interested in this curious place from this human's past. He also couldn't help but be fascinated by her.

"Back then, I was happy. My family was happy. Everything was different." She released the last bits of sand and wiped her hand off on her dress. "But things change and life moves on, right? No sense wallowing in it. I got through that, and I'll get through this, too."

He didn't know what she was talking about, but he could hear the quiver in her voice before she cleared her throat and straightened her shoulders.

"I've probably used up all my time already," she said, turning and giving him a smile. "But it's always worth it."

"You will be back?" he asked, not knowing exactly why he wanted to know.

"Always," she said. "And I guess I can count on you being here, thanks to my meddlesome friend. Not that I'm complaining. It was nice to talk to something other than the seagulls."

She started backing away, then seemed to change her mind, walking quickly back, dropping her shoes, grabbing him by the front of the Kranji uniform, and pulling his face down to hers. Her kiss was a shock, not only because it had been years since he'd been kissed by a female, but also because it was more aggressive than he would have expected from her.

Her tongue parted his lips as she moved one hand from where it had fisted his uniform to rake through his hair and pull him closer into her. She moaned softly, and he felt all the blood in his body rush south. As her tongue stroked his, his cock throbbed, and he wrapped both arms around her, lifting her off the ground. His body buzzed with need as he became almost dizzy from the taste and the feel of her, his head swimming as his tongue swirled with hers. Her soft body against his hard one felt more right than anything he'd ever experienced.

After a moment, she pulled away, and he lowered her back to the sand. Varden was breathing heavily, and his hands tingled from where he'd held her.

True stumbled back, touching a finger to her lips. "Wow. Ella really outdid herself with you."

"True," he said, his voice husky. He wanted to tell her who he was, and that he wasn't a computer-generated character created by her friend.

"You were just what I needed," True said, smiling as she backed away. "Thanks."

He watched her disappear through the door, his heart pounding. What had just happened? He wasn't sure, but he knew that—strange as it might seem to him—the reject bride was just what he'd needed, too.

If only she didn't think he was a hologram.

Sneak Peek of JINGLED: A Holiday Novella— Tribute Brides of the Drexian Warriors #7

Chapter One

Reina bustled down the corridor, her shoes echoing off the shiny floor as she took long steps. She touched a spindly hand to the bobbing blue swish of hair that extended over her head and sighed.

The human women were at it again.

As a tribute bride liaison, she was used to handling requests from the human females the Drexians brought up to the space station. It wasn't unusual for her to deal with everything from hysteria to disbelief to anger when the Earthlings learned they'd been abducted from their planet to be brides for a warrior race of aliens. Although most of the women eventually were happy with the arrangement—especially after they saw the hunky Drexians— Reina was not unaccustomed to drama.

As a Vexling—a species known for their attention to detail and desire to please—her instinct was to solve every problem and keep everyone happy. And she really did want her tribute brides to be happy, although sometimes she wished they didn't rope her into *every* scheme they came up with. She'd been involved in last-minute bridal showers, surprise weddings, and even something one tribute had insisted on called a "gender reveal party." Human's need to know the gender of their children so they could then dress them in certain colors baffled her, but she'd gone along with it.

And now this.

She reached the inclinator and swiped her hand over a panel to one side, waiting for a moment before the compartment doors swished open, and she stepped inside between a Gatzoid tapping away on a tablet, and a Neebix holding his tail in front of him.

The inclinator was crowded today, no doubt everyone busy as the space station got back to normal operations. It had been many weeks since the station—know by most as the "Boat"—had taken on new tribute brides or even allowed incoming transports of Drexians. The attacks by their enemy, the Kronock—along with sabotage of the station and the discovery of traitors within the Drexian leadership,—had kept them on high alert. Like everyone, she was glad things were returning to normal, although the latest request by the tribute brides was *not* normal.

"Reina?"

She turned and spotted another Vexling at the back of the compartment, his nearly translucent, spiked hair extending high above the other heads. Her pulse fluttered, and she hoped her gray cheeks did not betray both her surprise and pleasure at seeing Vivan.

"Greetings of the day to you," she said, extending the formal Vexling greeting, since they were in the company of so many others.

"Thank you," he said, as he wiggled his way to stand next to her at the front of the compartment that surged upward. "To you, as well."

Reina darted a quick glance at the fellow Vexling. Like all of her species, he was tall and lanky, although Reina had always thought that Vivan had a squarer jaw than most Vexling males. She knew he worked in the station's procurement department, determining what items were needed from Earth during the transports to the surface to obtain tribute brides. Vivan had often been the one to help her when her brides required something specific and did not want a holographic version.

The Boat relied on sophisticated holographic technology to create much of the fantasy settings for the humans, but some things could not be manufactured by light diffraction. That was why the space station had an entire department devoted to procuring specific items from Earth to make the human women feel at home. Since they were the key to the Drexian's survival, their happiness was paramount.

"You must be busy," Reina said.

Vivan nodded. "It has been many cycles since a transport returned from Earth. We are eager for its arrival." He focused his gaze on her. "You must also be glad to receive new tribute brides."

"Of course," Reina said, although she was relieved the brides would not be arriving that day.

Despite loving her job, she had welcomed the slower pace of things when the transports of the tribute brides had been halted. Her work partner, Serge, had grown increasingly impatient at not having a wedding to plan. She, however, had enjoyed getting to know some of her recent brides instead of having to immediately move on to the next arrival.

Vivan's large eyes studied her. "You seem worried, Reina."

"Not worried." She shook her head. "Perplexed. Maybe you can help me."

He took her hand. "You know I will always help you."

Reina knew her cheeks were flushing as the inclinator door opened, although she was grateful when everyone exited around them. She and Vivan did not step off. The doors slid shut again, although the compartment did not move.

"Reina?" His voice was quiet, but it made her jerk her head to meet his gaze.

All Vexling eyes were gold, yet his seemed more luminous to her. She swallowed and tried to focus her mind. What did she need to ask him? It had seemed important, but now she couldn't remember. *Think, Reina.* She closed her own eyes to shut out the distraction of Vivan's.

"Christmas," she said, her eyes snapping open.

"Christmas?" he repeated, tilting his head at her.

"A human holiday," she went on. "We've had tributes want to celebrate it before, but usually they did it in their suites. Now, a group of my brides want to throw a station-wide Christmas party."

"That sounds intriguing." He did not drop her hand. "What is involved in a Christmas party?"

"From what I can gather there is a lot of food, many drinks, songs called carols, and presents given out by a fat human man wearing red."

Vivan's high forehead wrinkled. "We do not have any fat male humans, nor do I think it would be practical to procure any."

"From what I understand, humans often dress like this fat man and use padding to look larger than they are."

Vivan's blinked a few times. "Fascinating. As long as I have been procuring things from Earth, I continue to be surprised by what humans enjoy. One day, I will have to tell you about the Slinky."

"I would like that," Reina said, jumping slightly as the inclinator doors opened, and a pair of Drexian warriors entered.

Vivan dropped her hand, and they moved to the back of the compartment, as the Drexians activated the inclinator and it rotated before accelerating.

"How can I help with this Christmas party?" Vivan asked in a low voice, as the Drexians discussed the Kronock.

"I don't suppose we have any tall, pointy trees on the station?" Reina asked, looking straight ahead.

"Do trees have something to do with the fat human in red?"

Reina tried to recall what Mandy and Bridget had said about the trees. Christmas trees, they'd called them. They'd both been talking so fast that it had been hard to make sense of it all. "I think the humans cover the trees with balls, and the fat man puts the presents around the bottom."

"This is very strange indeed," Vivan muttered. "I can see why you are concerned."

"The tribute brides want to have this Christmas party on the promenade in a week's time. I'd hate to tell them no, especially since some of them have been through quite a lot."

"I heard about the reject who was rescued from the Kronock hybrid. I am glad she is all right." Vivan glanced at her. "After all the things that have happened on the station, maybe a party would be good for everyone."

The inclinator stopped, and the two Drexians got off. Vivan also stepped off. "I should get to work before they send out someone to procure *me*."

Reina giggled. "Of course."

"I will see what I can do about these Christmas things," he said, giving her a small bow with his head before starting to walk away.

Reina shot a hand between the inclinator doors before they closed. "Would you come?"

Vivan turned back around. "Come?"

"To the party?" Reina asked before she could think better of it.

A small smile curled his gray lips. "If you will be there, I would not miss it."

Reina let the doors close and sagged against the walls of the compartment, her hands fluttering at her throat. Now she had more than the Christmas party to worry about.

To be continued...

———

Want to read more? Turn the page to order or read for free in Kindle Unlimited!

Also by Tana Stone

The Tribute Brides of the Drexian Warriors Series:

TAMED

SEIZED

EXPOSED

RANSOMED

FORBIDDEN

BOUND

JINGLED (A Holiday Novella)

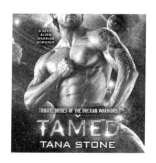

TAMED is now available as an audiobook! Listen on:

AUDIBLE

AMAZON

Acknowledgments

Big hugs to all the readers who have written me or messaged me to let me know you enjoy the Tribute Brides series! I love hearing from you! And I especially adore all the readers who have left lovely reviews. You are the BEST!

Special shout-outs to my fabulous SFR crew: Ivy McAdams, Hope Hart, and Miranda Bridges. Love navigating this wild ride with you three ladies!

My biggest thanks, as always, is to you, the reader, for reading my books. Writers would be nowhere without readers, so thank you!

About the Author

Tana Stone is the sci-fi romance author of the Tribute Brides of the Drexian Warriors series. Her favorite superhero is Thor (with Jason Momoa's take on Aquaman a close second), her favorite dessert is key lime pie (okay, fine, *all* pie), and she loves Star Wars and Star Trek equally. She still laments the loss of *Firefly*.

She has one husband, two teenagers, and two neurotic cats. She sometimes wishes she could teleport to a holographic space station.

She loves hearing from readers! Email her any questions or comments at tana@tanastone.com.

 facebook.com/tanastoneauthor

 instagram.com/tanastoneauthor

Printed in Great Britain
by Amazon